also by William Davey

Dawn Breaks the Heart
Howell Soskin, New York

The Angry Dust
Chinese Edition / Beijing
American Edition / The Wesex Collective / Colorado

Lost Adulteries & Other Stories
Carrefour Alyscamps / Paris / London

The Trial of Pythagoras and Other Poems
Alyscamps Press / Paris / London
Greek Edition / Perigramma / Athens
English Indian Edition / Parnassus Press / Madras

Bitter Rainbow and Other Poems
Carrefour Alyscamps Editions / Venice / Macclesfield
Greek Edition / Perigramma / Athens

Arms, Angels, Epitaphs and Bones
Rydal Press / Santa Fe

WORKS IN PROGRESS

Splendor from Darkness
novel ready for publication

The Angry Dust
French Edition ready for publication

Brother of Cloud in the Water

a novel by

William Davey

Edited by Susan Davey

The Wessex Collective, 2008

Brother of Cloud in the water © 2008 by Susan Davey

ISBN-13: 978-0-9797516-2-2
ISBN-10:   0-9797516-2-4

Published by The Wessex Collective
P.O. Box 1088
Nederland, CO 80466-1088

Web: http://www.wessexcollective.com
contact: sss@wessexcollective.com

Acknowledgments
Selections from the novel have previously appeared in *The World of English* (1992, vol. 2, in Chinese translation) and in *Lost Adulteries and Other Stories,* Carrefour Alyscamps Press, Paris/London 1997.

book jacket photos: *"Papua New Guinea Man Wearing Headdress"* (Corbis Royalty Free Photograph) and *"Sunset over the Sea, Kimbe Bay, Papua New Guinea"* (PureStock Royalty Free Photograph), both courtesy of Fotosearch

Printed by Thomson-Shore, Inc., Dexter MI

The Wessex Collective, publisher of progressive books:

If literary fiction (story telling) is the way that human beings can understand and describe what history feels like, we believe it should be relevant to universal and historic human experience. We believe also that literary fiction provides an opportunity to recognize, with significant impact, the problems of societies as well as individuals. At The Wessex Collective we are publishing books that demonstrate an empathy for human vulnerability and an understanding of how that is important to the larger society.

Contents

Chapter 1   7
Chapter 2   12
Chapter 3   17
Chapter 4   24
Chapter 5   36
Chapter 6   41
Chapter 7   55
Chapter 8   61
Chapter 9   73
Chapter 10   84
Chapter 11   92
Chapter 12   101
Chapter 13   108
Chapter 14   112
Chapter 15   117
Chapter 16   124
Chapter 17   136
Chapter 18   146

1

They call me Brother of Cloud in the Water. You know how people are, once they start doing something nothing will make them change, and people started calling me that ever since the day we went to the place called the Pool that Forgets.

It started this way. There were ten of us and we were the bravest there were. We had just come back from the enemy coast and we had nine heads. They were wrapped in big leaves, the ones that don't break, and we had vines tied around them in knots and they were comfortable to carry. Their mouths were facing our backs when we returned from the raid so their tongues would not tell the secret of our trail. The bleeding was over and we were no longer annoyed by the flies that had bothered us most of the way. They were fine heads. There was a child and a woman and seven warriors all told. But unfortunately we came to the cliff Where the River Leaps Down and under it to the side was the Pool that Forgets.

Let me tell you why. When we were children our grandfathers told us it was called the Pool that Forgets because when flesh falls into it the pool forgets to send it to the surface again. They said that sometimes wood comes up but wood floats in water better than bodies. So one time when we were no longer children and not yet men we seized the hunting dog belonging to the Man Who Hears Not and we made off with her to the Pool that Forgets. We threw her into the pool from the big rock above it and we waited to see her come up. We waited from morning till evening but she never came up. For two moons we went back and no one could see her and then we knew that the Pool had forgotten her.

Davey

But this particular day when we were returning from the raid everyone had taken a head except my brother. Maybe that was why he was talking when we were whispering and why he tried to sound as though he had no fear. When we reached the cliff Where the River Leaps Down my brother as is customary with us was forced to bring up the rear. That is the position of honor and dishonor according to circumstance. As an honor the strongest men are placed there to protect us against attack when we return from raids, but sometimes warriors who have not shown the strength to take a head are placed there in mockery to rebuke them for weakness. I think my brother understood this because as we reached the cliff beside the waterfall he ran ahead of us along the trail. He stopped at the edge of the great gray rock above the pool and stood there trying to look stronger than he was and then with a pride of tongue that such a warrior must always silence he dared to use oratory upon us.

"Hunters of Skulls!" he declaimed. "Warriors of the Only World! Watch me! I am not afraid of the Pool that Forgets."

And with those words he dove the length of two trees in the forest and he disappeared into the pool and we saw nothing more. We stared over the edge of the rock and for the time taken by ten calls of a bird we forgot the heads on our backs. They could have slipped sideways toward their own country or worse than anything backwards and the spirit of their tongues could have told their warriors the secret of our trail. But we kept gazing into the whirlpool until the magic of its circle swirling always in the same direction almost put us to sleep, and yet the part of us that remained awake was still surprised and displeased. Then a ghost entered my mind and drew my attention away from the force of the whirlpool sucking everything downward into a circle ceaselessly boring a hole in the surface of the water itself. I had seen my mother holding the skull of my father and my mother always spoke truth. Now I remembered what she had told me. "Your brother is full of envy. He is jealous of you," she said. "What is that?" I asked her. "It is something that happens to some men and women. It is something they have in common," she said. "Men and women have something in common?" I wanted to know. "Yes, three things," she told me. "Sometimes love, but always death

Brother of Cloud in the Water

and envy." Now I thought of that as I lay on my stomach with the spray from the waterfall dangerously wetting the string of my bow.

But our eyes continued staring into the circle of magic produced by the Pool that Forgets while at the same time our ears went on being deafened by the roar of the waterfall. Sometimes the gray pool began to turn blue and then it darkened to green but at last the foam mixed white into the gray and for a moment the whirlpool became white as the mushrooms of death that grew on our mountains. We had stayed like that for too long for all the time something dangerous was happening. The heads on our backs were slipping from the position of their mouths to our backs. The leaves and vines that held them had been loosened by the spray so we took the heads out of the leaves and faced them forward and cut their tongues out. Now we knew they could never tell where we had been or where we were going, but immediately one of the warriors asked me whether we should eat the tongues. I shook my head for I was not certain that we would speak with wisdom afterward.

We threw the tongues in the Pool that Forgets and we did not reach camp until after dark and twice we were almost killed by our own outposts. Although it was not my fault I felt responsible since it was my brother who had done that stupid thing. I have always had a reputation for wisdom but I became embarrassed to be the brother of a fool. For people have always asked me questions and I know they think I have wisdom because they listen. Sometimes people ask questions and you can see they do not care what the answer is. They do that to make themselves look important or to make another man feel important but they never do that to me.

The next day I returned to the pool and looked for my brother and still he was not there. Like the hunting dog, the pool had forgotten him. There was not much to do after the raid except to protect the trails and make magic with the heads so I went to the pool every day for almost a moon to look for my brother. Suddenly one day when I was about to leave I saw magic happen. Beneath me between two rocks something strange was floating. It looked like a great silver fish with the head of a man but without eyes and it was the color of a cloud from which rain never falls. My brother's skin had been the true color, the color of embers when they are cold and not gray like ashes, the color we all have, dark, beautiful. But this thing looked as white as a cloud or a maggot or the scale of a fish. It was my brother.

    The council of warriors considered I owned this magic because I had discovered it and the body creating the magic had been made by my mother. So I let the warriors who had been with him the day he dived from the rock see his body first and then the other warriors and last the women and children since everyone knew that stupid as he was he had done a magical thing. He had made the Pool that Forgets remember to bring up its dead. The women must have seen this on our faces because they began to sing and then the men started to look serious for they suspected that soon they would have to honor a fool who had become great. And what would we do if someone suggested bringing him ashore? Too much greatness is not comfortable and I knew in my heart he would be bad magic and I was certain he would bring more water to ruin our bowstrings and recklessness into our councils.

    Above him a cloud moved slowly away from the sun and in the spray of the waterfall a rainbow formed over his body and at last it disappeared like a Bird of Paradise in the shadows of the forest. But I still stood there listening to the women singing, "See him! Oh, see him! He looks like a cloud in the water."

    And the women were right. Not only had he come back from the Pool that Forgets but he had changed his color also. I watched the women picking flowers and weaving them into wreaths and I saw them tossing the wreaths toward my brother but their wreaths fell into the Pool that Forgets and not so much as a flower came up. Then fear seized me for something told me that my brother was changing from the object of magic into a god and no sooner had I suspected that than all the women turned toward me in order to praise me for my association with a fool who they now showed signs of wishing to treat like a god and with a new deference and the desire to honor me they started chanting and calling me Brother of Cloud in the Water.

    I have borne that name ever since and told no one I hate it. But

Brother of Cloud in the Water

that day I was thinking fast and I said, "Listen to me, People of the Only World. Hear me!" They all became quiet and I said, "Does one try to bring a cloud to land? A cloud should come and go as it pleases." Then I persuaded them to splice two poles together and I pried my brother loose from where he was wedged between rocks and as he floated away toward the place where the big fish eat everything the women sang and the children tried to run after him along the bank of the river.

My brother was gone but my name has remained and the reason I am lying here on the moss and talking to you is that you are a Forest Spring to whom I intend to tell my story. I am far from old but nevertheless I am wise and a wise man does not talk to a river. Who wants to talk to a river which never stays to listen and which moves so loudly that a man cannot hear a word of his own? But a spring will listen and so I have wedged the shaft of my spear into the roots of the tree that grows above you and after I have uttered these words which are rare as sunlight coming through leaves in the rain forest then I will let my canoe drift on the waves in the Lake of the World and I will jump at last into the water among the fish who eat everything. But first I should tell you why. This story is not about my brother nor is it about my name. This story is about the Bird of Ghosts. The story is also about the Woman with Hair the Color of Blood.

2

It began strangely. One hundred and twelve moons ago I was on the Mountain with the Back like a Pig and it was dangerous because I was all by myself. There was not a cloud in the sky and the sun was bright and burned your eyes unless you looked through a leaf. Along the top of the mountain huge trees were growing and that was unusual because where there is rock there are never many big trees. I had the feeling that something magical would happen and I sat down with my back against a rock and the sunlit stone began to warm my spine. I watched some blue lizards running over the smooth surface and then I heard the buzzing of flies and I saw the lizards stop. I waited to see them catch the flies with their tongues but suddenly the lizards seemed to have vanished. Their skin had turned gray like the stone.

Below the mountain our camp and the camp of the enemy were covered by clouds and the tops of the clouds were white and blinding and they reflected the light of the sun. To the people below they might have seemed gray and without light but high on the mountain where I was sitting the dense air separated me from the earth and I knew that the white clouds below me and the yellow fire from the sun were spinning a web of enchantment that had caught hold of me and from which I did not want to escape. Far away I could hear the faint sound of a waterfall and as I listened to it a bee with wings of gold and eyes the color of rubies began humming above the motionless bodies of the lizards. Suddenly a lizard lunged at him but the bee zoomed upward and the lizard fell back on the stone. The sound of the waterfall mingled with the buzzing of the bee and finally the insect circled back above the lizards with no regard for himself as he went on staring at me through eyes which seemed about to drip red liquid. When it finally flew away the lizards slowly turned blue again and their eyes became as green as the leaves on the tops of the trees nearest the sky and I began to feel sleepy for I knew I was in the center of a circle of magic and so I stretched out on the ledge of warm stone and although it was dangerous I let myself fall asleep and my spear slept in the palm of my hand.

There was such deep magic in that land of strong sunlight and blue lizards and bees with eyes of fresh blood that while my flesh slept on the stone my head began to dream. I dreamed that a bee had brought an enormous hive through the air and other bees had clustered around him and together they made such a shattering noise that the lizards darted away and were hiding under the rocks. My dream told me that this vast humming in the air held a secret I would never learn in my sleep.

I sat up with a start. Above me the bee had turned into a brilliant bird with wings which seemed longer than the tallest tree in the forest. Then I knew I was in the presence of a spirit because my hand did not tighten on my spear but instead I gazed at this featherless creature sailing above the clouds and flying closer to my sunlit mountaintop while sending from its silver throat an interrupted roar like thunder. And as I watched, the huge bird drew a wide circle over me of which I was the dot in the center and above this motion was the calm blue of the sky. At last it flew in a smaller circle and for an instant I thought I saw men between its wings. They might have been warriors but I made no plans to fight nor did fear come upon me. You will never guess what I felt. Joy! Instantly I knew I was favored and that this special spirit bird was going to light on my mountain and show me wonders in this land where an enemy always has arrows.

I could not believe my luck: somehow I had known that new magic would happen before the sun went down. I went on watching its movements, for like other birds which continuously circle in a clear sky, I knew that this magical one was searching for something. It dropped lower and lower until it became obscured by the trees but once or twice through a thin patch of leaves I saw sunlight flash from its great silver body as it prepared to light on the long ridge of the mountain. Then its voice became silent and I found the silence disturbing for I was standing spellbound waiting to actually witness the presence of a great spirit.

Suddenly I heard a tremendous sound of trees being severed like twigs and part of the forest was wrenched from the stillness of living and hurled downward with such force that the broken trunks bounded upward, hovered momentarily, and then fell back again to the earth. I stood listening to wood being ripped into splinters with its strands hanging by white threads and while my ears echoed with the crashing death of the trees I almost imagined that later I would hear them talking with the creaking voices of ghosts. But this thought lasted only an instant before a gale of leaves swirled around me with the force of a storm and through its top I saw a sea green sun shining.

My hand was on my spear but my body remained motionless. Trees had hurled past my head and branches weighing more than all the men in my tribe had shot over my shoulder faster than arrows but all that had touched me was a storm of leaves. And as I waited for this spirit of silver to turn into red fire and at last into blue smoke and to ascend again into the sky he had come from so that he could once more disappear into space, with a slowness I had not expected after the swiftness of such violence I became covered with dust by an emerald wind made out of moss blown from the trees.

I had been too amazed to move but now I turned my head sideways and far below me I saw entire trees that had been hurled over the mountainside with a strength I had never before encountered. The black crown of cassowary quills I was wearing had been swept from my head but the tusks of sacrificial pigs were still on my arms and all that had happened to me was that I had dust in my eyes. I rubbed them with my knuckles and there in a clearing in front of me with a steak of green on its injured side I saw the bird resting as though he were still alive. Bright rays of sunlight glittered from his hard skin and behind him I glimpsed a long scar of white wood where his power had torn through trees like a spear through flesh. Everything was strangely still and as I waited once again I heard the sound of the waterfall.

I knew that soon I would see what a spirit looked like and though it might be useless I took my spear and went forward to the place where the head of the bird was resting on the ground. The skull had been opened but unlike ours it was a skull you could look through and I saw many skull fragments scattered over the stones and their edges sparkled in the sun and looked almost like light on the cresting of waves. But my hand seemed not to belong to my body because it tightened around my spear when I saw two warriors sitting inside the skull. I crept toward them with my spear ready until I realized they were not warriors. They were victims. They were sacrifices to the power of this Bird of Ghosts.

I began to think it was boastful to brandish a spear in front of two sacrifices made by an ancient spirit and so I turned my spear upside down and I crawled inside the skull and stared at them. They were dead like all sacrifices. Their necks dangled forward and I lifted their heads and looked into the sockets and I was going to put their eyeballs back so they could interpret the dream of the future but I could not find them. The men were strapped into harnesses that had held them secure in their passage to death and I saw they were wearing brown skins with white fur reddened by blood and beneath the fur that covered their chests loops of ruptured intestines lay in their laps.

At last I walked past them and once more amazement came over me. For I admit I had expected to find order and arrangement better than men's ceremonials or the battle plans of warriors. But obviously this spirit did not care. Instead he had thrown everything together and axes had broken from boxes and underneath the mass of crates and containers lay a strange white sand.

After a while my feet became sticky and I saw little ants that love anything sweet begin crawling into the bird and start eating the sand I had stepped in. I touched it and put my finger to my mouth. It was sweeter than yams. Then something told me that the Bird of Ghosts had brought me a sign like a bent twig on a trail. He was telling me that he could kill more trees than lightning and that he could make

Davey

men's eyes come out of their skulls and at the same time he was saying that he was sweeter than yams. He was saying he could bring gifts even to ants and instead of twigs he had made a nest out of trees and laid it at the feet of Brother of Cloud in the Water. I could not believe my good fortune.

    And now I knew what to do. I would tell my tribe about the Bird of Ghosts because we had no magic like him and our magic brought with it nothing you could touch. I would tell the warriors how the Bird of Ghosts descended from the Blue Tree in the Sky where some thought the Bark of Beginnings had grown and how instead of rain or lightning he had brought us axes and even sand you could eat. So I searched through the bird and found other boxes and I tore the covers off and inside were many small rectangular slices of a brown substance and as I held one I felt it melting in my hand. It left a fragrance on my fingers and I tasted it and it had more scent than the sand. I sat in the middle of the bird and ate pieces of the brown food and paid no attention to the ants climbing over my skin. At last I stood up and crawled through the skull of the Bird of Ghosts and went outside in the dying daylight. Far away I heard toads singing and I saw the white eye of Night rising above the horizon.

3

I sat down on the trunk of an uprooted tree and stayed like that for a long time. Then I started thinking that my people knew me as their strongest warrior and the only one who had taken thirty-two heads. They thought of me as the husband who had not married again after the death of his wife because he was in love with the dead. They knew me as the warrior with the most wisdom and they had long known I was a headhunter not a cannibal. They also knew that I was the best hunter and that through the carmine color of the poison berries I alone could always see the red eye of the crowned pigeon glowing like an ember in the fire. And since I had no wife to work for me they knew that I had been forced to make myself rich and inside my carved coffer in the men's house were Bird of Paradise feathers and ivory hornbill beaks and pearls I had pried from fresh waters guarded by landlocked fish whose fins like to breathe the air. But no one dared steal from me for they knew that soon afterward the relatives of such thieves would be forced to smear the gray clay of mourning over their bodies.

As I was thinking this I was conscious too that an honest man must be dishonest. It is not his thinking but the thinking of the world that makes him so. Like a pack of hunting dogs on a lone outsider a tribe will turn on a man who reveals thoughts that are different than theirs. I am therefore silent and my tongue never tells all my thoughts, but now I knew the Bird of Ghosts had backed me against a cliff and I could not observe this magic and continue to cover myself with the shame of silence. And then as though to bring my attention to the strength of his sorcery below me the clouds

Davey

began to fade away and after a while only the mists were left and at last they too were lifted into the vastness of night and the forests beneath me became flooded with starlight. And as I gazed at it I knew that such clarity happened only during the day and it was the sun who drew the mists up from the muck where the leeches sucked the russet leaves in the water until they could find flesh. I raised my head and looked above me at the surf of stars breaking over the reef of night and never had I seen them rolling toward daylight with such a bright foam of brilliance.

The next morning I went back to the bird and I emptied a box and put axes in it and sacks of white sand and the sweet brown food and as I did so I discovered something else. I tore off its skin and underneath it was silver like the bird but I could not crack it. So I chopped its top off with an ax and inside I found salty red flesh that was good to eat. I took many of those also and the box became so heavy that I hid my spear in order to carry it. I did not return on the trail that I had taken but went straight down the cliffs and many times I almost fell and the box almost fell with me. When I reached the forest floor a cloud of blue butterflies hovered ahead of me and went on drifting in the direction I was walking. Then the silence of their flight was disturbed by a Bird of Paradise calling and the butterflies veered away from the call and flew toward some flowering vines and I knew in the sunlight they were no longer afraid of the bats hanging upside down in the hollows of trees.

As I approached our camp I gave the recognition grunt of a cassowary but despite this signal I heard the cough of a blowgun. Immediately behind me in the python mushroom circling a tree a poison dart struck and quivered in the hard jelly of its flesh. I was forced to call out my name and finally our youngest warrior stepped from the green fringes of a shadow fern and I went forward and wrenched the blowgun out of his hand. I took an ax from my box and chopped the blowgun into four pieces and dropped them at his feet. Then I followed the smell of smoke into the camp and soon I was surrounded by sniffing dogs. I saw the heads of women peering out of their huts and one of the tethered pigs tried to eat the slime of frogs from my feet where it must still have been clinging from all the wading I had done in the morning among the pools of the forest.

Suddenly I kicked the pig in the snout with the heel of my foot. I was in a bad mood and I seized some thatch and covered the box from the Bird of Ghosts and sat down and waited for the men. I saw them wander out of the men's house and begin to sit down in a circle around me and no one seemed interested in the box for along with them came the strong odor of tobacco they had been smoking. I knew this was a bad beginning for a tribe who even shows interest if women catch spiders to eat and I sat there saying nothing, but I was thinking that I had been greeted by a poison dart and a pig had tried to root on my foot and now no one wanted to know what I had. Then the thought occurred to me that perhaps I should return to the Bird of Ghosts and put his gifts back inside him and wait until night when the four stars that are crossed into arrows of warfare appear in the sky and tell him the truth which is sharper in darkness that as a bearer of battle scars it was my duty to declare that he had landed on the wrong mountain.

This thought was interrupted by someone asking where my spear was, but I started to frown and no one else dared ask me another question. We sat there in silence and at last from the huts all around us, though still retaining the silence of respect, we became slowly encircled by women and children. A warrior moved forward and put a log on the fire and moved unhurriedly back again.

When everything was motionless I decided to speak.

"People of the Only World," I said. "Hear me! I have found a bird larger than all our huts. The sun flashes from his silver feathers and inside him he has magic and food."

Then the same man who had asked me where my spear was now demanded to know what kind of bird that was and he said maybe that it was the bird of a dream. He was wearing bracelets and necklaces and he stared insolently at my battle scars while he sat on a pandanus palm with one hand resting lightly on the rough wood of the trunk. I became angered and I reached inside the box and pulled out an ax and with one motion I slammed the ax into the log on which he was sitting and the ax cut through the loose bracelet of sea shells he wore around his wrist and though the ax stopped quivering his sea shells went on falling into the dust.

"Does that look like a dream?" I said. And then I stood up and pulled the ax out of the wood so that he could not claim the ax as his own and I gave it to a warrior and again I opened the box and took out three more axes and gave them to three other warriors and I kept no ax as my own. This lent me prestige and I saw in the men's eyes how pleased they were with the axes. I brought out the sweet white sand and the dark food that melts and no one would touch them and I ate some of each but still they drew back from food they had never seen and I heard them muttering that maybe such food was taboo and not food but magic and that the white sand inside their bodies might turn inside out like a bêche-de-mer and become once again the heavy brown sand of the beaches. The women were more fearful than the men and I heard them saying that to bear a child in the belly was burdensome enough but to carry sand in your stomach was too heavy. "No! No!" they said with a sound that was almost like wailing and instantly their children started to cry.

"Do you agree with the women?" I asked the warriors and they were silent and did not say no. "Then if the food sent by the Bird of Ghosts is full of the bad evil you fear then so are his axes," I told them. "Give me the axes and I will take them together with the food and give them back to the Bird of Ghosts and tell him the people here are too stupid to enjoy what lies in front of them except for the bite of a snake."

I held my hand out but no one put an ax into it and then one of the warriors stood up and took a piece of brown food and held it over the fire. Immediately the food melted in his hand and fell into the fire and it seemed to infuriate him that he stood there holding nothing but still his fingers were sticky. "Fool!" I said. "You do not cook the body of a ghost. You eat a ghost raw like a fledgling. Do you think a ghost is the hand of an enemy or a pig for a feast?" And once more I ate the brown food in front of him.

A small boy broke loose from his mother and I gave him a piece and he swallowed it and then the mother cried out, "You have poisoned the labor of more than nine moons! How will you give me back a boy who is dead?" And I saw the warriors watching him while the mother clutched the boy by the hand to keep him from entering the long ground of ghosts. But the boy lived and the mood of the people changed and suddenly I became something larger than the Brother of Cloud in the Water. I became the sorcerer who had found the gifts of the Bird of Ghosts.

The next day my tribe moved out. We left only the sick and the old people to keep the pigs from the gardens and we walked under the green gloom of the rain forest and then onto sunlit hillsides and some yellow butterflies drifted in front of us and the children tried to catch the butterflies in their hands. When we reached the sheer rock of the cliffs we pulled ourselves upward by the branches of shrubs and the woody lianas dangling from trees at the top. Finally we came close to the place where the Bird of Ghosts had been lying.

Everyone knew it was the lull before magic and we waited and did not climb the last knoll. The sun was shining and under the mountain on the Lake of the World we could see blue water and waves with white crests but further away a black squall was gathering and sheets of rain began falling into the water. From the forests below us only silence ascended but now not even the sound of an insect could be heard on the mountain. Slowly an eddy of air sent a leaf drifting downward from the top of a tree. At last we crept up to the edge of the knoll and there lay the Bird of Ghosts with its hard feathers reflecting the sunlight into our eyes while the sacrifices remained sitting inside the skull. A murmur of awe came from the warriors and when it died down I heard once more the sound of the nearby waterfall splashing.

We told the mothers that any child who entered the Bird of Ghosts would be thrown into the Pool that Forgets so the women and children stayed at a distance. I retrieved my spear for I had no way of knowing if, during my absence, a sorcerer had turned magic from the Bird of Ghosts backward. It might have become a Dragon Bird. I opened a string bag I had lugged with me and had some of the warriors put kau-kau under its wings as a food offering. Some of the more brave men kneeled down and looked under its tail to see if the Bird of Ghosts were male or female. Then we crawled into the

Davey

skull but this time my hand tightened upon my weapon. The lips of white men were now red and it seemed as if the sacrifices were talking, but as I got closer I saw swarms of scarlet ants eating away at their mouths and my hand relaxed on my spear.

The warriors and I moved many boxes from inside the bird and we hid them in the shrubs at the edge of the cliffs. I told the men if enemies discovered our boxes that we could steal up behind them and kill them with arrows and those who escaped would have to run into our spears or jump to their deaths on the rocks below. We found things that my interpreter living with our outposts behind the beaches told me were what white men call clothes. For despite our row of skulls on mangrove stakes warning them away from the beaches some white men still come ashore from ships and they have corrupted our outposts who now wear clothes instead of brown bark pounded soft and green leaves sliced in strips and bright feathers or necklaces of white and orange shells which sometimes cause death if touched before drying.

We spent one night on the mountain. The children were beginning to cry from the cold and concealed by the shrubbery our enemies could have discovered us. So the next day we descended and we carried with us as much as we could and for more than a moon we kept climbing the mountain and carrying away boxes of food. The people were happy and they forgot my old name and began to call me Brother of the Bird of Ghosts. I was glad I was no longer named for a fool but I knew the sole reason for happiness was that I had discovered a power stronger than sorcery. This strength not only could level the trees of a forest but it brought with it powerful gifts.

We made thirty trips and removed all the food but we were not alone in consuming something which came with the Bird of Ghosts. Masses of red ants went on eating the faces of the sacrifices and slowly the faces started to turn into skulls as inside the clothing the bodies resembled skeletons which still had not whitened with age. But the nights continued to be cold on the mountain and we knew it was magic that the fur of their clothes went on warming their bones. Near the dead bodies many beetles lay in black mounds and then we understood that the beetles too had tried to eat the flesh but the ants had stung them to death.

    Though we took away many things we left all the boxes with what white men call bottles. You could look through the tops of the bottles and see brown fluid inside them. The fluid was the same color as the food we had eaten and two of the warriors told me the fluid was a water spirit of the brown food that melts. They wanted to drink it. But I looked at the bottles and they were decorated with skulls and the long bones of men. I decided to leave them. I told the warriors we took our own heads and we never had the need of the heads taken by others. Besides, I was certain that the liquid inside the bottles was like the liquid venom of snakes and if we left these snakes of death inside the Bird of Ghosts they would protect it.

    We took everything else and then we slaughtered a pig and feasted and drank kava and the husbands went off with their wives and the children were excluded from the huts and they played games together under the paradise palms. Everywhere I went people called me Brother of the Bird of Ghosts and though I am not sure a warrior should ever be happy I felt like the highest leaf on a tall tree growing in cleaner air than the mists of the forest and sensing the warmth of the sun turning it green in the daylight.

Davey

4

I should have known that this was the time in stories of things which occurred in days brought back only through dreams from the ancestors that a man must expect good deeds to turn into bad and truth like the head of a snakeskin pulled toward its tail to be turned inside out and end up as lies. For not more than six moons passed before the people started to taunt me and they demanded to know why another Bird of Ghosts had not landed on their mountain. Then the man with the bracelets went around whispering that I had lost my magic and despite all our gifts he persisted in hinting that my Bird of Ghosts was only a dream and one day he said so while the men were chopping wood with my axes. But no sooner had he started to whisper that I had been blinded by dreams and my thoughts had been dazzled by witchery than I knew I could not let him continue because only women are witches. And through no fault of my own but through the cleverness of his tongue he had put me into a position I could not accept. For without an act of revenge which showed justice was with me I would have lost face simply by listening while he went on sneering at the Bird of Ghosts with his clever insinuations.

"Look!" he said, and he took an ax from one of the warriors cutting a tree near a river and he hit it against a boulder. The sharp blade of the ax broke off and all that was left was a wide dull part still on the handle but with which you could not even cut a vine. Then he laughed. "Does that look like an ax of a great ghost?" he asked and once again he gave a laugh of contempt. Then he dropped the ax and the first warrior let it lie on the leaves. He knew it was useless.

Brother of Cloud in the Water

"Why didn't a magic ax split the stone?" he demanded of the silent circle of men. As he turned toward me he picked up his spear and I heard his new bracelet of shells rattle against the wood while even in shadows under the trees the sharp teeth of bats on the tip of his spear looked white in the gloom of the forest.

But instead of directly confronting him I put down my own spear and walked over to pick up the ax. The men realized I was ruined unless I did something but they also understood that revenge does not always occur in an instant. I held the ax to my ear and I could see the gesture surprised them. No one looked more startled than the man with the bracelets.

"What are you doing?" another man asked me.

"I am listening," I said.

"To what?" he wanted to know.

"To what the Bird of Ghosts tells me," I answered, and though they continued to ask me I remained silent and carried the broken ax back to the village. But the next few days I remained watchful for I knew that the man with the bracelets would try to kill me. At last I slipped into the woods with the broken ax and a shell. I separated the creepers with which I had concealed a hollow in a tree and inside it were my blowgun and darts. Wrapped in banana leaves to protect it from moisture, a section of bamboo capped by another rested upright within the trunk. The bamboo contained a poison which can paralyze pythons. But I did not want my enemy to die so I found a forest pool and I broke off a twig and dipped droplets of water into the shell from the twig. Suddenly I was splattered with water by something plopping into the pool, and, ignoring the interruption, I returned to the tree, took a clean stick and mixed the poison in the bamboo container. Then I stirred the water inside the shell with the stick. I dipped two darts in the water and looked overhead for some sunshine and at last I dried the darts in a ray of sunlight slanting down from the trees.

I washed off the stick in the pool but beneath the scum almost as soon as I started I saw a white shape in the water. With his belly upward a dead frog rose through the dense scum to the top. His wide mouth was open and floating in front of it was the long yellow tendril that had been his tongue. Silently I told him I had not intended to kill him and I felt regret that I had not been more careful. His death was an omen and so I covered the tree with the creepers and returned to the village.

Half a moon went by before I reported a tree python with the length of six men. The warriors wanted to eat his tough white flesh and make drums from his green skin. I told them whoever found it should give six calls of a Bird of Paradise and others should instantly come to the calls. They agreed and I added, "Don't worry if you don't find the python. This one has skin of sky blue. So if you find magic instead of the snake, give the calls anyway."

They nodded and I watched them disappear into the forest. I stayed behind and shadowed the man with the bracelets, but he did not come near the tree with the hollow and I had to go forward to get my blowgun and darts. It took me a long time to double back and shadow him again and when I did I noticed he was taking old trails. I was tired and once more I had to travel twice his distance but finally I managed to hide myself in his path. I crawled into a thick thorn bush and I left blood on the points of the thorns. I waited while he walked toward me and I remember thinking that he was not serious even in his hunting. He did not give the bush a second look and I saw he did not suspect an enemy would wound himself to accomplish a purpose. I knew he would never expect to find me in such a place and I had a good shot at him. Quietly I braced my elbows on the thorn branches and then I shot him in the stomach.

A surprised followed. He pulled the dart from his stomach and went on walking toward me. It was like a bad dream. I thought I had mixed too much water into the poison and as I watched he staggered over and leaned against a tree. With my second dart ready I did not leave the thorn bush until I saw the bow fall from his hand. At last I stood up and after cutting the string of his bow, I broke both his bow and his arrows.

He was still standing, slumped against the tree, and silently I stood beside him. The strange thought came into my mind that we must look like two friends. He tried to look at me but the muscles of his eyeballs seemed to go in different directions and would not come to a focus. Suddenly his jaw went slack and his mouth fell open and he startled me by an immense roaring of breath. In ripples without rhythm along the sides of his body I saw his muscles flutter like a wounded bird.

Then he fell with such suddenness that again I started with surprise. He had fallen on his face in a mound of dry leaves and as I listened to the strangling sound of his breathing, I saw that the storm of air roaring out of his lungs had managed to stir only one leaf. His right leg drew up in a tight contraction while the muscles on his left leg became seized by more rippling motions which now looked like a river discharging into a rising tide. I would have felt sorry for him if I had not known that he would kill me if he could. I was certain that speech would enter his ears with its echoes overlapping but I decided to say something anyway.

"I'm not going to kill you," I told him. "I'm going to teach you not to speak badly."

Rolling him onto his back, I took my knife of cassowary bone and cut his tongue out.

I turned him over again on his stomach so he would not choke in his own blood and I cleaned my knife and put it back in its sheath. Being certain that I was not observed by others, I hid my blowgun and darts in my favorite hollow tree and returned with the ax. I took his tongue and placed it on the broken blade of the ax and wrapped them both in mimosa and tied them with fern fronds.

I washed my hands and went back toward the village and when I reached the clearing I gave six calls of a Bird of Paradise. After a while I heard the warriors running and they arrived close together and the first man asked me, "Did you find the python?"

"No, but I found magic."

"What sort of magic?" he demanded.

This was the day I had waited for and this time I asked them, "Do you remember when I listened to the ax?"

"Yes," they said.

"And do you remember I did not mention what the ax told me?"

"Yes," they repeated.

Davey

"Do you also remember how the man with the shells said the ax from the Bird of Ghosts had no magic?"

They nodded with eagerness.

"And have you forgotten how he broke the ax on the stone?"

"We have not forgotten", they exclaimed.

"Neither have I. That is why you should know what the ax told me. It said 'I can no longer cut wood but I can still cut flesh'. So come and I will show you its magic. It has cut someone's tongue from his body."

They followed me into the forest and no one looked at the man with the shell bracelet for first I went straight to the ax and they watched me remove the mimosa and there was his tongue still lying on top of the broken blade of the ax. After a while they went over to him and rolled him onto his back and stared inside his mouth and then they could see that his tongue was gone and that in truth the tongue was still bleeding on the tool he had unnecessarily damaged. I knew they would pick him up and carry him into the village and so I suggested that they carry his tongue and the ax blade also.

The next day we held a council and we decided to smoke the tongue to preserve it and tie it to the broken blade of the ax with the tough webs of warrior spiders and keep them taboo in the men's house as reminders of the magic of the Bird of Ghosts. Already we had a man who could not hear and now we had a man who could not speak, but the warriors said before a moon he would die. I said nothing for I had a feeling that he would go on living the way mushrooms do without as much green as a dead leaf. And I was right for a sorcerer cured him by placing bitter plants in his mouth and hot stones on his stomach and in two moons he was well.

After I learned he was well I had some planning to do and one evening I waited till twilight when no one likes to walk in the forest and when the daylight was turning to dark. Overhead in the trees cuscus were beginning their barking and disputing and even though I smelled them their stench never interrupted my thoughts for I was thinking that the Man Without a Tongue had received a lesson and it was no longer intelligent to exclude him from our councils. I knew that his life had lived in his tongue and though we should not honor him for the stupid use he had made of it we should perhaps avail ourselves of the intelligence of his silence.

So we discussed it in his absence and I suggested that as long as he did not shake his head or nod or make gestures with his hands and as long as he remained completely still then we should include him in our councils and his opinion which would never be known would count along with ours.

Then one of the younger warriors asked, "What good is a council like that? What good is a council one cannot hear?"

But I spoke sharply and I told him that speech was often more stupid than silence and I asked him what speech did we hear from the skulls that we still thought were worth hunting. And he replied angrily that everyone knew the skulls represented ghosts and ghosts talked to us when we were sleeping.

"That is true," I said, and I picked up a skull that still had its jawbone. "Do you see a tongue in here?" I asked him.

He said he did not, so I told him to go outside and make the Man Without a Tongue open his mouth.

With the quickness of annoyance he stood up and walked outside. But when he came back I instantly asked, "Well? Did you see a tongue?"

He said there was no tongue to be seen.

"There is no tongue to be seen in a skull," I reminded him.

Then I told the warriors that what we now had was something we had never had before and this strange new thing was the daylight silence of a ghost who yet wore flesh but could not make us dream because he was still alive.

So from that day he sat in our councils and I spoke for him in the hearing of his ears and I knew as far as he was concerned that never again would I need to fear anything from him. I believed that his anger at being bested and his desire for revenge would be absorbed by a vanity which would agree with us that only a god could inflict such an injury on him. And I turned out to be right and for five moons afterward the people kept calling me Brother of the Bird of Ghosts and I had gotten rid of my worst enemy without killing him.

Then without warning something else happened that I had not expected. The thought had not occurred to me that the ghost I had found could be endangered by children. But when the rains ended and the ground dried the children were freer to play in the village and their mothers watched them running with arms outstretched and listened to their cries echoing throughout the camp.

"Look at me," a child cried. "I'm a bird."

"Look at me," another called. "I'm a bird of silver."

With their arms dipping and swooping they pretended they were birds.

"Look at me," called a child who was bolder than the rest. "I'm the Bird of Ghosts!"

Holding his arms as though they were wings, he took a leap and went sailing into a shrub and landed on his stomach. His mother ran toward him and picked him up because she thought he was injured.

"Don't touch me!" the child cried. "I have magic inside me."

Pulling away from his concerned mother's grasp, he ran away with his arms still outstretched, dipping and gliding as though he were a bird, and I saw a smile come across the face of the mother.

But now that I lie on green moss and now that a spring is the only one hearing my story and now I have reached the conclusion that I am the only hunter who can kill the quarry I still call myself, I am able to look back and see things I had not noticed before. It has taken the stillness of a forest spring to make me understand that the smile caused by a child was the beginning of the end. For now I see clearly that the wives told their husbands what the children said and they must have described the mimicry of the children's actions pretending to be birds and finally the men's amusement made them refuse to believe that the Bird of Ghosts was still something more serious than the object of childish play. It was then their half-concealed mockery became open doubt.

"Where is the next Bird of Ghosts?" the men persisted. "He will not come down from the blue shining. Your Ghost has deserted you. You are not the brother of a ghost. You are only the Brother of Cloud in the Water! Your Ghost has gone further away than your brother and all that remains is an empty shell on a mountain."

"No. That is not all that remains," I said.
"What else is there?" they wanted to know.
I looked at them coldly. They had had good luck and good magic. Maybe now they deserved the bad.
"The liquid food," I reminded them. "The food you wanted to drink. The food marked by skulls and the leg bones of men."
"That is true," they admitted. "We forgot that."
"It's still there. Remember I thought it was dangerous?"
"Yes. You said not to drink it."
"I can remember my words. But now I am hearing your words. And your words say that the Bird of Ghosts has no power."
"Yes!" they said loudly. "His power has gone."
"Well, then, the Bird of Ghosts has gifts that you have not tasted."
"True," they agreed.
But then they began again and they kept on asking, "Where are new gifts from a ghost who has many? Why does a ghost from the sky light on earth only once?"
I could not promise to find a new Bird of Ghosts on another mountain. There was not a word I could say and so I remained silent but inside me anger burned that nothing had been enough for these people. I was as silent as the Man Without a Tongue and indeed we stared at each other with unexpected sympathy.
"Why don't you say something?" one of the warriors asked me.
I was holding an arrow and suddenly it broke in my grip.
"You have broken your arrow," the same warrior said, stating the obvious.
I continued my silence but as I looked at him I remembered that this was the man who had one of my axes. I remembered also that all of them had eaten the brown food and the flesh covered by small silver boxes which the Bird of Ghosts had brought down from the sky. Their wives had eaten it. Their children had eaten it. But now they had criticisms. Now they had complaints.
I seized a bundle of spears and my bow and arrows and walked toward the door of the men's house.
"Where is Brother of Cloud in the Water going?" I heard

Davey

someone ask.

The night was dark and my eyes were dazed from looking into the fire and I stood waiting until I could see the trunks of the trees. Then I walked into the forest. Rain began falling and I covered my bow with the bark of my cape. It was cold rain and clean and it dripped from the leaves and washed the smoke from my hair.

Far away on the River of Madness I heard the white man screaming. He had been washed ashore from a wreck and we had found him pacing up and down near a river. The warriors had wanted to kill him and take his skull back to camp, but before they could do so I noticed his eyes still gazing upon the river as though in a sorcerer's trance. Then I knew it was more than a desire to drink and I thought that inside his brain the pollywogs of this veneration for water would hatch into frogs that would sing with insanity and if the warriors tasted this man's flesh like our cannibal enemies liked to do, his infection would enter them also.

So we had carried him further away from the sea and we turned him loose on the same river and again he waded into the water and started screaming. Then the warriors backed away from him because he had become taboo. We let him live along the river and though now he weighed less than a child he still wandered naked upon the banks of the river looking with the intentness of madness into the water and when it rained he screamed. Sometimes we left taro root on the path his feet made in the mud but when we went back we found he had refused to eat it as he followed this ghost in the river that he alone could see.

I stopped abruptly. I had almost walked into a tree from which a dim but pearly light was glowing. Impulsively I placed my hand on the bark and instantly a black space appeared on the trunk and then in the darkness my palm turned the color of a pearl. I had been absorbed by my thoughts. I was thinking that we kill off the children with madness who are born in our tribe and so madness is never among us. But as I listened to the man's screams I began to wonder if madness, like a mountain swept clear of clouds by a windstorm, might loom behind wisdom and be the demented answer of our forefathers to the terrors of life.

This worried me and I was glad when the rain ceased and silence spread through the forest. Then white moths started flying into the tree trunk that went on glowing with the light of pearls. I found a tangle of tree roots and I leaned against the trunk and waited for daylight. There are times like that when night lasts forever and you doubt the sun will come up in the sky. I had not had many but a few are enough and until now it had been the death of my wife that had caused the wakefulness of those nights without end.

But now I had another such night and this time the Bird of Ghosts had caused it. For deep inside myself I had no idea what to do. I had walked away from the warriors' questions because I did not think they should have been asked. I was wondering also how many times I could fight. Could I fight my own tribe as well as the enemy and also keep white men from landing on the shores I had always defended? There was a limit on how many tongues I could cut from the mouths of people who delighted in doubt.

I slept the short sleep of a man who has not solved things that he must and when I awakened the sun was shining on my eyelids and the light made my lids move upward and for a moment I was blinded by sunlight. But no sooner had I shut my eyes to avoid the brilliance than I opened them again because a furry cloud had covered the sun. The cloud was close to the treetops and though no breeze was blowing my ears heard a windstorm of squeaking and rustling and then the stirring and drifting down of leaves.

It was a flight of flying foxes which had been feeding on fruit in the night and were now in the daylight returning to sleep in the trees. Toward my spear hand I noticed four trees without a leaf on them and even in shadows cast by the other trees I saw they were dead but from their boughs reddish clusters of fruit still seemed to be hanging. I had found a refuge where the flying foxes had rapidly landed and hung upside down to rest inside their folded wings and wait for twilight to send them aloft in a windstorm of chittering until they circled and settled on fruit trees to the south.

I stood up and started to walk toward the mountain. But for once I had no plan. I did not believe that in returning to the place where the Bird of Ghosts rested that the magic of some answer awaited me.

Davey

Before when I had taken a game trail a purpose had gone along with me and as I hunted I had been accompanied by hope. Something different went with me when I hunted enemy warriors and I had not thought of this till now because it is not wise to reflect on actions from which death will result. But suddenly I realized that when I hunted men I had been accompanied by such a tight expectancy that it coiled inside me like a snake ready to strike. Now I had neither of these things.

At last I reached the edge of the forest and I turned to look back at the dark green pools and oozes of slime in which on my approach schools of tadpoles had started to wiggle. I was thirsty but I did not want to drink from the murky pools. I knew also that I had not finished a thought. For if the snake of expectancy accompanied a man into warfare with other men, what name could I call it that directed my steps toward a mountain where I would never utter a wish? I was not going there to receive an answer for I was not asking a question. The mountain had already provided the greatest magic that had entered our world.

These thoughts had gotten me nowhere and for a moment it was a relief merely to look around me. Beyond a heavy thicket of bamboo I saw boulders and bright pebbles and a clear stream cascading down the mountain and its ripples ran swiftly over the shallows. I lay down on the small rounded stones and drank and drank again. I had started to wonder if I had been given an omen. Perhaps the false red fruit with its sharp claws clinging upside down from the death of the trees was a sign telling me that something would be upset. As I climbed the smooth face of the rock leading to the ridge I grasped the branches of shrubs growing from cracks in the stone and after a while an odor of resin from the leaves crushed in my fingers rose to my nostrils despite a breeze rising from the valleys and blowing now toward the top. A wispy series of transparent clouds as separate and lacy as mimosa leaves tried unsuccessfully to dim the sunlight and I looked above me to see if they would drift together and form a cloud that would cast a shadow. Instead a vulture sailed through them as dark and distinct as he was in the sunlight and when I looked once more the clouds and the bird had disappeared and the stone ridge

Brother of Cloud in the Water

and the evergreens on the mountain lay once again under a blue sky.

The breeze died down and everything was silent and at last when I looked over the rock at the edge of the ridge the silver body of the Bird of Ghosts was reflecting its rays. Along the whole mountain the sun had warmed the stones and I began to wonder why no lizards were darting and stopping and trying to catch flies. I placed my bow on a warm rock to tighten the bowstring after the damp of the forest and I lay my arrows beside it. Now I could hear the buzzing of insects and again it seemed strange to me that nothing was pursuing them. I was still holding my spears, but then I sat down and I put the spears down too and kept my left hand on them. Below me the blue waters of the Lake of the World stretched far away, but from the meeting of sea and of sky a lavender mist obscured the horizon where I saw a black storm gathering. Then a snake of wind and spray grew out of the storm and swayed like a cobra and his whirling motion sucked water out of the sea.

I had the peaceful feeling of distant violence. I continued to listen to the usual sounds of the flies buzzing and I watched them light on the rocks. They were toad flies and they tilted themselves forward and lifted the greenish gold of their bellies up toward the sunlight. They spread their transparent wings and I glanced through them and saw the stone underneath.

Before the Bird of Ghosts had landed I had let myself go to sleep on the mountain but this time I continued to keep my hand on my spears and I decided to remain awake.

… Davey

5

I had made a lucky decision for soon afterward I began to have the sensation that something was watching me. I did not believe I was being spied on by men and the situation made me uneasy. Then a ghost from the dead left lasting darkness in time to give me a warning. I was grateful for this intervention and I remained without moving until the shadow of a cloud drifted over the mountain and onto the rock. Then I turned my head slowly and although I saw nothing again I had the impression that something saw me. The cloud passed and stillness surrounded me and the only things moving were heat waves shimmering over the rocks and rising and vanishing into the air. I continued to turn my head slowly but I still noticed nothing except bright flakes of mica flashing with sunlight from the gray stone in front of me.

Then from behind a rock something moved toward me and a great forked tongue fell heavily from some large mouth and was sucked swiftly inside again. "Aiih!" I said silently and I asked myself if the tongue belonged to a new kind of snake. I had never seen a tongue like it, one with a notch so deep that both sides drooped. I remained motionless while I tried to remember. Pythons lived near water in the heat of the jungle and I wondered how this snake could stand the cold of the mountain. So with my right hand I took one of my spears from my left and I drew my arm back and then I cursed myself for a fool. Rather than the tiny eye the color of ashes which belonged to a python, not more than ten steps away through a crack in a towering stone I realized that a great golden eye had been watching my movements. Again the huge tongue flopped forward

Brother of Cloud in the Water

in front of the rock and was sucked back once more while with a calm alertness the lidless eye went on stalking me. I have only the patience of men and I knew this animal would outlast me, so I crawled forward to confront it.

Suddenly I heard a tremendous hiss and I came face to face with a creature I had never before seen. It was more than the length of two men together and heavy as five of our warriors. For an instant I was immobilized and as I stood there its size grew double when it inhaled. Its mouth, shorter but wider than a crocodile's, opened deliberately and I saw inside it curved teeth that could hold a boar. When I saw its claws sharper than bamboo splinters but broad at the base and longer than a man's fingers then I knew its claws were as dangerous as its teeth. I had confronted a warrior animal.

Framed by the alert but golden calm of its stare, its mouth seemed not to know the warm trance of its own eyesight for suddenly its tongue withdrew from the rock on which it had been slowly twitching and a sharp hiss came forth as its jaws snapped shut faster than a brown tree snake striking. Like a crocodile it preferred to look at me with one eye only and I saw that the skin of its body was the color of dried mud mottled by large beads in red circles. Behind it rose a towering wall of stone and on both sides were steep slabs of sunlit rock and without trying I had left this dangerous animal no retreat.

I stood there holding my spear behind me but my weight was forward. I knew if I stepped back that I could not throw my spear with the force I now had and I also thought that if I moved the animal would attack me. Suddenly the creature thrashed its heavy tail and some pebbles were swept violently away and then the slap of an echo reverberated among the rocks. I did not wait for it to thrash that tail again. I hurled my spear with all the strength I had. Piercing the heavy skin, the spear head went through its body and with a hiss like a cry the creature turned its huge head sideways and bit the end of my spear in two.

I jumped to the top of a rock and with its curved teeth still holding the shaft of my spear the animal jumped also. It leaped at me and I drove a new spear through the top of its head but the spear broke in my hand as though it had hit a skull made of stone. The broken spear told me I was going to die so, still holding my other spears, I climbed a tree as fast as I could but the creature climbed up after me. With nowhere to go I leaned back and rammed a spear through the eye closest to me. Deliberately it turned its head and gave me a brief serene look from its other eye which was the color of the tail of a Bird of Paradise and slower now its tongue flicked forward while behind its claws shattered bark and strips of wood went falling downward.

Now I knew what this being would do. It would seize me with those curved teeth and with its claws it would open my stomach and claw my liver away from my flesh. My liver would fall to the rocks beneath me. Then I noticed a long vine and holding my spears in my left hand I quickly grabbed it with my right and swung away from the tree and over the cliff. But the vine returned toward the tree and as I approached the trunk I heard another sharp hiss when the animal thrashed its tail and hit me flat in the chest. I still had my spears but my breath was gone and I had been knocked away from the tree and sent swinging out over the rain forest where below me the trees looked smaller than shrubs.

Again I started to return and intentionally I loosened my grip and slipped down the vine so that I could land with my feet on a boulder. I could feel the heat from the whipping tail mark burning into my skin and the bones of my chest ached. But instantly the animal backed down the tree and at the bottom of the trunk it balanced itself on its tail and then swiftly turned on me. For a split second I had a glimpse into his soul through his serene golden eye which seemed to hold purpose without anger but its mouth was open to kill me and it ran toward me faster than a warrior. As I watched this warrior disguised as an animal I was not surprised that my own feet started running but that they were running toward it. Inside me a dam of fury had broken and I shouted, Aiih! You! and threw a spear in its mouth. The point wedged in its throat and with the deliberateness with which it did everything again I saw its tongue flicker slowly as it drooled a sticky saliva. Its body was bristling with spears but it waddled heavily toward me and with each decisive step its pointed claws clicked on the hard surface.

Below me I saw a ledge of rock with a large stone lying on it and I jumped down twice the length of my body and landed beside it. Without regard for itself, the animal lunged toward me and it fell heavily onto the rock. I picked up the stone almost the weight of a warrior and brained it the instant it landed. I was gasping. Upon us both the sun was shining and far away I heard the musical cooing of doves. Then as slowly as though it were preparing for sleep the creature coiled itself sideways and its legs relaxed and its body sagged between them. But it kept its one eye open staring at me with aloof calm even though death was approaching while with the detachment of a dream its legs twitched like a dog's sleeping. It seemed to enjoy dying. Perhaps it had done this before and knew where its spirit belonged. But it took me a long time to control myself. My lungs were heaving, my ankles were swelling, and there was no skin left on the palm of my hand. I slumped down beside the animal. Its single eye with the same golden light of alert calm still watched me from its sleep. It was dead.

Much later I too fell into the exhausted sleep which follows a successful battle but as I slept a part of my mind was still awake and I saw myself like a stranger rising from the side of this huge animal sleeping near me with its tranquil delight in death and I watched myself honor him by not cutting his head off as was our custom in warfare between men. Instead I honored him by leaving him untouched, a warrior animal greater than myself, who had suffered the bad luck of falling on stone more heavily than I had only to be at a disadvantage in battle. Then my dream told me that I must place around him a circle of stones with an exit place for his spirit. And I asked myself whether without dishonoring him there was something I could keep from the most deadly encounter I had ever had and which despite its deadliness contained something as surprising as one finds when a huge tree falls in the forest and one sees suddenly that within its branches furthest from the ground a golden orchid had been growing.

Now another sensation began to come over me and I dreamed that green swallows were flying above me and their feathers were

Davey

falling out of the sky and settling on my face. I was asleep but I brushed their feathers away and when I awakened I imagined I still saw their green feathers descending. I sat up suddenly and as I did so a gust of wind detached a leaf from a tree growing above me and the leaf drifted down and landed on my chest. As I threw the leaf away I turned to look at the creature still sleeping beside me. He was covered with leaves and angrily I brushed them off him. Fresh breezes were blowing around us and I stood up then and encircled his body with a ring of stones and as in my dream I left the one place open for the escape of his spirit. The glaze of death had started creeping across his earthly vision and suddenly an unexpected sadness came over me. I almost regretted that this warrior animal with a heart stronger than mine had because of a chance encounter been turned away from daylight toward the long nighttime of ghosts. I remembered how violent he had been and yet I knew that he would not have delighted in killing me any more than a wave rising from the sea delights in sweeping away people and palm trees and the sand on the beaches. I wondered as I looked at him what ancient world he had come from where death was no different than life.

6

I watched the crimson circles on the warrior animal's gray hide fade like blood shells left on salt in the sunlight and they turned at last to a pale rose. The wind went on blowing and I brushed more leaves from his body but as I did so I noticed that the middle claw of his left front foot had been broken by his fall. Then I knew I could keep that claw without offending his spirit and afterward I would have about me the magic of his strength. So I tried to pull the claw from its foot but it was held by a tendon tougher than the root of a tree. I drew my knife but the tendon resisted and I sawed with the knife till the sweat formed on my forehead. At last I severed the tendon and then I wrapped his claw in the bark of my belt. I wanted to leave that place where death was the same as sleep and I climbed out of the rocks and back on top of the stone ledge from which I had jumped.

Suddenly a warm wind swirled around me and I was surprised by its stench. It smelled of crab mounds and mud snails in mangrove swamps and the rotting sea wrack at ebb tide. Below me the forest seemed to be swaying and dead leaves and dry twigs started blowing past me in the air. I stared down at the Lake of the World and I noticed that the clouds which had been on the distant horizon the day before had kept their shape and were driving the snake of wind ahead of them and already it had begun to whirl the sand from the beaches.

As I watched it the mass grew to the size of a giant python and its thrashing tail began ripping the trees from the swamps and wrenching the grass from the tussocks. Around the whirling motion of its tail a cloud of sand followed and finally the tan color of the beach fell away and was replaced by black mud from the river bottoms. The hot wind blew steadily and the writhing motion like an emerald python did not follow the direction of the wind but twisted anywhere it wanted. A green pall began to cover the sky and behind it the sun shone like a light through moss. Fresh scents of eucalyptus leaves blew up the mountain but again they were followed by stagnant odors of slime swirling in the air and choking clouds of fungus swept from beneath dead bark. A green gale blew living leaves through the bare branches where the flying foxes were sleeping and then the wind turned red with fur and the storm sucked many of the flying foxes up and destroyed them. Below this gale of green leaves another tempest of ochre bark and gray twigs was following. Forked lightning struck and my ears were deafened by a sudden thunderclap and two hot raindrops fell on my forehead.

Then I remembered my bow and I ran toward the rock on which I had left it. Surprisingly the bow had not moved and my arrows were still lying beside it. As I leaned down to pick them up I was buffeted by a blast of wind and I dodged between two rocks and staggered. Again lightning struck around me and once more my eardrums were almost shattered by the nearness of the thunder. I braced myself and held on to the stone as best I could. Then the wind started howling louder than our dogs sometimes do when they are feeling sorry for themselves, and gray shapes coiling and stinging themselves were carried over the mountain. I asked myself if this were a dream for a cloud of vipers had been blown straight through the air as though they weighed as little as dust. A red piece of bleeding fur suddenly dropped in front of me and as I raised my eyes I saw the Bird of Ghosts. It was as still and untouched as my bow had been on the stone and with the lofty detachment of skeletons the two sacrifices were watching the events as though they had never existed.

Then a strange weak wind began blowing and it was warmer and not as strong as before and I felt that this viper was draining the strength from the air. I turned around and watched its writhing body advancing and then I understood that the snake of wind had not been dancing on its tail. Now I knew that its mouth had been in the sea where it had been swallowing waves and as it left the water and turned on the land its jaws had dislocated the way pythons can when they eat pigs and it started to swallow entire parts of the forest. I realized that its judgment was erratic and that it would leave behind a bow that weighed nothing and arrows which weighed even less but next to them it would suck up a tree taller than the heights of all our warriors and that tree would dissolve in its stomach quicker than the flight of a spear.

Deep booms of thunder increased and flickers of lightning as delicate as butterflies veered back and forth from black clouds. Above the storm a white cloud formed and sunlight gleamed from its bright surface. Beneath this towering whiteness gray streaks tinted with inky blackness merged and separated, their edges fringed like ferns. Holes appeared in the tops of clouds and then other clouds drifted into them and the massive darkness cast an immense shadow over lighter clouds under them. Thunderous sounds echoed inside them and the tiny butterflies of lightning still flitted through them from one cloud to another.

Between the peals of thunder I heard a roar of continual crushing that sounded like an avalanche of stone falling down a mountain. I crouched between the rocks and wondered where I should run but something told me it would be like running from a flight of arrows into the falling of spears. A man must make his peace with things and I told myself that there are worse places than stone if your spirit is to leave your body. And once again I stared at the Bird of Ghosts and I saw its skin reflecting the lightning the way it had sunlight and I gazed at the skeletons and more than ever they seemed to convey the contempt of death for the noise and violence of life. Their silence suggested that beyond sunlight which festered the flesh with decay that there was a region of starlight reached only by allowing this decay and after one turned into bones which were almost as hard as the rocks that the change was a triumph and a warrior should not regard it as loss.

The branches of thorn bushes whipped round the sides of the boulders but I had a magic thought and for a moment I felt nothing while I ceased to watch the greenish mists of leaves and slime that accompanied the whirlwind twisting its way up the mountain toward the top. Above me the heavy bough of a huge tree gave a splintering crack but I was still listening to my thought telling me that I could become a sorcerer of the storm. I was thinking that if I ran from the rocks and entered the skull of the Bird of Ghosts and sat down next to the skeletons and if the storm lifted the Bird of Ghosts into the air and turned it to silver dust then my flesh would become red dust inside it and together the dust would shine like a star one sometimes sees at night glowing with red silver magic.

My leg was itching and surrounded as I was by the immensity of the storm and the probable approach of death I was surprised by the smallness of the sensation. Blood was trickling down my leg and for some reason the itchy feeling was more uncomfortable than the sight of my blood. I had not felt the thorns which had whipped from the bushes and were embedded now in my skin. I pulled them out one by one but the wind whirled the thorns from my hand before I could throw them away. A tree of lightning grew suddenly out of the ground and its branches shot over the mountaintop and over other mountains behind me and for an instant my sight was seared by the brilliance just before the thunder rumbled around me and the stone trembled under my feet. Far away a serene line of blue was revealed behind gray clouds and then was obscured again.

A new gust of wind flattened me against a rock and when it slackened I heard the fall of a boulder crashing down the stone face of a cliff and finally the sound was extinguished by the silence of the forest. Sand from the beaches preceded the whirlwind and as the storm twisted toward me the wind of sand hit me like a blow. Above the whirlwind dark clouds projected and then black rain fell so hard I could not raise my eyelids and a pool of mud fell from the sky and hit the stone beside me with a heavy muffled slap. The gray daylight deepened until the clouds of mud lumbered away from the mountain and collided without merging over valleys in the distance. I watched the weight of the clouds resist downdrafts from the valleys which were sucking the mists that accompanied the clouds toward the river bottoms and cleared of the mists the clouds seemed blacker and at last they moved heavily off. Wind screamed up the cliffs and whined over the stones but were then followed by a hesitant silence interrupted with distant whisperings of thunder. The wind had died to a breeze and the unnatural lull made me as uneasy as the storm. Slowly a scarlet hibiscus blossom floated through the air to my feet.

I decided to run for it and still holding my bow I made a dash toward the Bird of Ghosts and sat down next to the skeletons. Inside the Bird of Ghosts I had an unexpected feeling of being apart from the violence and I shared the calm of the ghosts as we watched the wind destroying more trees. It twisted its way toward the rocks where I had left the warrior animal and I touched his claw still wrapped in the bark of my belt. Simultaneously with a loud crack I watched a bolt of lightning run up a tree faster than the warrior animal, splitting it as it went, and I knew it was the tree we had both climbed and in which he had almost killed me among the lianas and vines. I lifted my head and then I saw the tree sucked upward with such force that it disintegrated and was turned without fire into a smoke of white wood. The smoke blew off the cliff at the edge of the mountain and with the tree went the vine that had saved my life.

The strength of the wind was too great to allow the rain to fall, but the storm whirled off the edge of the ridge and then I saw its grayish green coil writhing its way up another mountain. Dust started to settle and I shielded my eyes with my hands and after a while I could feel grit on my teeth. Laden with dusty powder a blue butterfly which had survived the storm drifted heavily downward and lit on the shoulder of one of the skeletons. I watched him try weakly to move and I leaned over and blew the dust from his wings, and as if he were still unafraid of the wind but had been alarmed by the violence of my breath, he flitted away from me back toward the shelter of the storm.

Brown raindrops fell on the skeletons and I heard heavy drops of water splatter on the Bird of Ghosts but then the dirty rain clouds drifted off and thin gray clouds replaced them. Something bright lay on the floor and as I picked it up I was surprised to see that like a clear pond it reflected my face but when I touched it the surface was dry. My hair had turned green from the dust of leaves that the storm had crushed in the forest. Rifts in the light gray clouds started to open and behind the rifts a background of blue sky appeared and from it rays of sunlight slanted downward. The sunlight cast shadows from the brows of the skeletons into the empty sockets of their eyes. Fine weather was approaching.

    I crawled outside and when I stood up I saw blue water on the Lake of the World and as though the storm had never existed sunlight glittered from the waves. The howling screams of the storm had been replaced by stillness and as if every creature had been blown elsewhere not a sound came from the forest. The cooing of doves could no longer be heard and the flapping of rock pigeons' wings had become as quiet as the rocks themselves. In the sudden silence the only thing audible was the blood pulsing in my ears and I stood for a moment listening to the disturbing throb of my blood. Without focusing my eyes I was staring ahead of me as if there were something I had forgotten and then I remembered the warrior animal and I ran toward the rocks. I looked up to where the tree had been and as I lowered my gaze I saw that nothing was left and the animal had vanished along with the tree. I sat down on a stone and put my elbows on my knees and tried to comprehend the meaning of this giant storm. It had swept away the warrior animal that had tried to kill me but I regretted his departure and I asked myself whether I had an ancestor who could tell me from the ashes of death if I had murdered an animal who was someone I should not have touched.

    Thoughts are ghosts of things and sometimes they destroy the people who do not escape from their company. I remained influenced by them only an instant longer. Then I climbed from the rocks but along the ridge I saw a wide expanse of blue water and it looked as though the whirlwind had sucked up part of the sea and poured it upon the mountain. I walked toward it until I noticed that it glowed with a sheen brighter than cresting waves. It was an entire field of dead butterflies swept up by the storm and dropped on the mountaintop where rays of sunlight were being reflected by the blue brilliance of their wings.

    Above the butterflies the sky turned orange and the dark shapes of the departing clouds took on the reddish brown color of earth. Toward the setting sun long strips of white clouds became as crimson as blood and then the light brightened and tongues of sunlit flame leaped outward in straight streaks and after awhile they darkened and faded to dull red like dead hibiscus flowers. Suddenly I was startled by the first sign of life.

Swifts who had survived the storm had flown out of their caves into the twilight and in the still air high overhead they were swooping and hunting insects. As I watched the sky I realized there would be no moonlight to descend the cliffs and that I would have to spend the night in the Bird of Ghosts. I knew I had nothing to fear because no enemies would be able to raid with their trails destroyed by the storm and when the cold breezes started blowing once more I entered the Bird of Ghosts and as I walked further inside I was surprised to feel sand under my feet. Some eddy from the whirlwind that had hit me with sand when I was crouching between the rocks had blown it inside and left it lying like part of a beach. It was very comfortable to lie on and I quickly went into a dreamless sleep.

It seemed only an instant later that sunlight challenged my eyelids. Then I knew it was morning and I had slept through the night. I was starting to stretch myself when I stopped suddenly. Near me on the tiny beach sucked off the seashore by whirlwinds and dropped on the mountaintop by the power of the storm the coils of a sand adder were quivering slightly as he settled more comfortably into the sands. I knew he did not want to move in my direction and the odd thought entered my mind that like myself he too had just awakened. I did not wish to confront him with a gaze and so I glanced instead at his short thick body covered by coarse gray scales. The sea sand in which he coiled half hidden was finer than his scales but I knew this snake disliked the sea and that grains of sand in upland savannas that had formed in rivers long ago gone dry were exactly the same coarse shape as the scales at which I was now glancing.

There is never enough time for things that are important. As I lay near the sand adder I felt how good it was to have death near at hand but not intent on killing me. I wanted to remain on the sand with death looking at me through the eyes of an adder even though I knew that the world would soon force me to emerge from a state in which I was content to avoid its activity. But I was stubborn. I remained without moving. For the sand adder was gazing at me through the oddest eyes I had ever seen. In turn I decided to look at him with sympathy for his huge head swollen by poison glands seemed to me to indicate a forgotten curse laid upon him by some sorcerer among his ancestors which impelled him sooner or later to strike the life around him. And as though to prove this true his tiny eyes gave me a look so meek and full of odd apology that if I had not known he could kill me I might even have smiled.

For a long time we lay in the sand looking at each other, he being direct while I was indirect. I regret I do not know what he thought. As for me I wondered also whether he wore that look as though he should excuse himself for things he had done because through a transformation of ghosts he had once been a warrior in the past of the world who had killed so many men that now he felt he should excuse himself for the mountain of skulls he had left upon the plain of battle. Near me, I decided, disguised as a snake, lay a great warrior who had become sickened by the world.

I rose carefully, backing away as I did, and as I left the Bird of Ghosts and walked slowly into the morning light I asked myself if some part of my past was lying behind me half hidden in the sand. The field of dead butterflies still lay on the mountaintop but the undersides of their wings were now facing the sunlight and today I noticed no reflections of brilliant blue. A breeze started wafting the stink of swamps sucked dry and acrid oozes from crushed plants into my nostrils and never had I smelled an odor like it. No higher than my spear a thin wisp of cloud drifted over my head and immediately the air became fresh and good to breathe. I inhaled it deeply, hoping it might replace the dust forced into my lungs by the storm. After a while I heard the silver skin of the Bird of Ghosts begin to creak in warm sunlight but what surprised me were the other sounds.

For after the noises of most twilight times, the frogs piping in trees, the shrieks of animals caught in the claws of the charcoal owl, the chirping of crickets emerging from leaves on the floor of the forest, and the sound which made even the hair of a warrior stand up on his spine—the cry of the woman bird being killed by a tree snake—all these sounds died down in the usual morning stillness.

But this morning was different. Around me I heard the cries of birds trying to locate each other after the devastation of the storm. And as I stood listening to the unexpected bird calls, a song as flowing and beautiful as a small stream rippling over smooth pebbles began to ascend the cliffs from the rain forest far below me. Then the song was interrupted by a harsh challenge and above the forest the air seemed ripped aside by a sudden swoop. It was a sea eagle diving.

The ugly shrillness of his cry faded as the eagle rose and circled slowly and sailed at last downward. Air currents carried him toward the Pool that Forgets but when he came to the waterfall where my brother had died I saw the eagle still with wings outstretched sail suddenly higher until he became a black dot in the sky. Then waves of strange laughter entered my ears and I walked to the edge of the cliff. A laughing bird like the others was calling for his mate, but as I stared at the cliff below I told myself that he would be right to laugh at someone who had no wings. For the vines and lianas attached to the trees had been wrenched away by the whirlwind and nothing was left but stone. I decided that this was the moment to leave and holding my bow in my hurt hand I descended the cliff very slowly. I was thirsty and weak from hunger and I took my time and did not try to hurry.

When I reached the clear stream from which I had drunk the day before I lay down again and started drinking. I was so tired I had not looked at the water. Then I felt something clogging my mouth and I spit it onto the stones and stared downward. Lying among the gray pebbles was a red piece of bat fur. Disgusted, I began my walk back to the village while part of my mind kept wondering whether I should shoot something to eat. But I did not need to shoot anything because the dead bodies of animals killed by the storm were lying around me near the uprooted trees. I could still taste the wet bat fur and I decided not to eat but to wait till I got to the village. It was difficult walking because I had to climb over fallen tree trunks and avoid the thorn bushes that had been ripped from their thickets and now hung stiffly impaled everywhere. Bright rays of straight sunlight were streaming into the forest from new holes left overhead by the fallen branches and they dazzled my tired eyes with such brilliance that I stepped into what I thought was a small pool but instead I sunk down to my waist. Under slime which had turned the deep green color of shadows, a fin rose through the scum and something swam forward and tried to bite my knee from my leg. But its eagerness made it bump me and I scrambled onto the root of a large tree and looked downward.

It was a brown shark no bigger than a boy but vicious and hungry. As I stared at him I realized that the whirlwind had lifted the shark from the River of Madness and dropped him here in a forest pool. Sharks like this could live in fresh water and now I knew why he was still alive. But it offended me that my world had been turned upside down for never before when stepping into forest pools had I needed to defend myself against sharks. The thought irritated me but I remained motionless.

Suddenly the shark rose halfway out of the water and lunged violently toward my foot. A wave of anger suffused me and swiftly I seized an arrow and placed it upon my bowstring. Then I withdrew it. I knew the skin of the shark was so tough I would only ruin my arrow. I stood still, thinking. Then I jumped off the root onto dry land and looked around me. Bigger than a rat, a dead bandicoot lay beside a mangrove branch ripped from some swamp near the sea. Behind its long thin nose its skull seemed indented and I imagined that the storm had brained it against the branch. I laid down my bow and arrows and then I cut some creepers and tied the bandicoot to the end of the branch.

I was still angry and I jumped back on the root and dangled the bandicoot above the shark. He lunged for it but I lifted the bough and he fell back into the water. I drew my knife and opened the belly of the bandicoot but only a few drops of blood seeped out. I shook the stick and the intestines of the animal started to slip from his belly and at last some orange blood began dripping into the green water. Suddenly the pool seemed to boil and the thrashing tail of the shark covered me with slime. Then I leaned forward and dipped the bandicoot in front of the shark and the bandicoot and the bough vanished and at that instant I jumped into the pool.

But this spot was even deeper than the first. I sank to my shoulders in the water and at the same time I was hit on the ear by the stick. The shark had turned toward me as I dived under the green gloom of the pool and seized him by the tail. Again he twisted toward me but I wrenched him the other way and it seemed to me that the struggle took a long time. I kept sinking into the mud and the violence of the fish surprised me. He thrashed his long tail with slow force now because on the other end he was also moving the weight of a man. I had never expected that this would become a deadly struggle but his strength kept hurling me under the water and when I came up my eyes were covered with slime and above the pool I saw only a dirty green daylight. I did not know that my hands and my face and the inside of my arms had been rubbed raw by sharkskin and that I was bleeding into the water. Then the shark seemed to redouble its efforts and with an impersonality that I did not expect a part of my mind told me I was about to be killed by a youngster.

Suddenly under my feet I felt a firm flat root and with both legs I raised myself halfway out of the water. No sooner had I done so than I knew the shark had his greatest chance for instantly I felt his body curve inward toward my feet. I was still holding his tail and with a last effort I lifted him straight out of the water into the air. For a moment his jaws went on snapping while bits of green moss fell away from the remote look in his eyes. Then his jaws remained open but his tail began thrashing more violently and the convulsive strength of his body made me stagger as I struggled to hold onto his tail. At last I managed to drag him out of the water and I pulled him up on dry land and dropped him on top of some leaves.

When I released him I jumped out of his way because I was certain that even out of the water he was still a killer and I expected him to hurl himself off the earth and twist in another half circle toward me and try once again to bite my foot off. Instead, nothing happened. He lay still as a stone. I sat down near him and leaned back against a tree. I was trying to catch my breath and I wanted to watch him dying. There are some deaths you want to watch and his was one of them. Although I thought him to be very ugly, I was surprised to find myself thinking of the most beautiful animal I knew. I was exhausted. My skin was bleeding a watery kind of blood and there was a strange taste in my mouth coming up from my lungs that was sweet and salty at the same time. I lay down at last and listened to my breath wheezing. It sounded as though there was water in my lungs but I did not remember swallowing any water in the pool and I did not know why my lungs seemed to bubble with fluid. I sat up again and the bubbling ceased and then I went on with my thoughts. There was nothing about that shark to suggest anything beautiful and I could not understand why I was reminded of a Bird of Paradise. Then a childhood memory entered my mind and I wondered whether the memory had something to do with a difference in dying.

For one day in the forest when I was still a child but capable of hunting birds I had shot a Bird of Paradise with a tiny bow and arrow. I had been elated as I watched the beautiful creature fall from a frangipani tree. Around me I smelled the sweetness of perfume wafted from the flowers of the tree and eagerly I rushed forward to pick up my prize. But I had only wounded it and as I approached the bird recovered from its wound and uttered a long call filled with melancholy and surprise and pain. I had never heard anything like it but I recognized it instantly. It was the sound of departure. The bird was saying goodbye to the world it loved. I was stricken. I could hardly move. But I was not to be let off so easily. The bird did not oblige me by dying. Instead, on the fragrant leaves under the frangipani tree, it hopped in a circle away from my arrow as though it could escape death. I saw its orange eye focused upon me and I felt that the bird was seeing me for what I was, a murderer of beauty. Its head as golden as the sun at noon turned away from its wound while on the wounded side its wing went on beating against my arrow. I stood there transfixed at the sight of death. But some things cannot go on forever and I knew I must finish what I had started. I lunged for the bird and when I caught it I strangled it in my hands. With its turquoise beak it tried to bite me but it could not close its mouth as it took a last gasp of air. I dropped it on the forest floor and it lay on the leaves with its feathers the color of sunset.

At last I understood why I now hunted these beautiful birds with a blowgun. Poison is impersonal. As a child I was saddened by the death of beauty and now I knew why I had thought of the bird while looking at the shark. There are some deaths one wants to watch, but others are too painful to contemplate and like a cross current in a river the ugliness of the shark had brought back the thought of the bird lying on the leaves with a stillness it now shared with the shark.

An exclamation escaped me and swiftly I walked to the shark and seized it by the tail and slung it over my shoulder. This was a day for surprises. For suddenly the jaws of the fish snapped shut with a strength that jarred my spine and vibrated through the bones of my pelvis into my knees. I dropped him swiftly. I had been lucky not to lose the muscle at the back of my calf. Now I knew this death would take a long time and even though my patience was fading along with my strength, I waited while the shark thrashed on the floor of the forest. After a while I forced a mangrove stick into his mouth and behind his long front fins tipped by black markings I tied the stick with vines from a scarlet creeper.

Then I swung the dead shark over my sore shoulder and started walking toward the village. I still thought our sacred house guarded by skeletons and masks of madness had survived the typhoon and though I could find no trails I recognized after the destruction of the trees I walked in what I knew was the right direction. A pair of parrots followed me high over the treetops and they were shrieking with rage. They acted as though I had done them an injury and they kept circling above me, screeching. I had a glimpse of the green underside of one and the blue underside of the other and I told myself that this was a mating pair whose nest had been destroyed by the storm. Green thickets of bamboo were growing ahead of me but the wind had bent their tops downward and now the slender leaves had formed dim but greenish arches through which from time to time some interrupted sunlight slanted.

I was pushing my way through the thickets while the shark's fins kept catching on the canes when a black cloud drifted across the sun and underneath the arches of interlaced leaves I watched the daylight becoming obscured by the darkness. At last I got through the thickets but my shoulder was raw and I felt blood running down

Davey

my back. No hunter likes to return empty-handed and so I kept the shark on my shoulder as I went on looking for the trail. For the first time I began to wonder whether the village had vanished along with the trees which had been our childhood landmarks. But then I smelled smoke and at the same instant I discovered that the trail was actually under my feet.

7

I walked into the village with the dead shark slung over my shoulder and children still excited by the strangeness of the storm ran out to greet me with their fat puppies trotting behind them. But a pack of thinner dogs began trailing the fish and suddenly their leader leaped forward and bit the shark in the head. I heard a howl before I turned to watch him run away with his mouth bleeding. Two men came forward with a rattan rope and they threw the rope over the branch of a tree and tied it to the tail of the shark. I felt as though I had no strength left but I helped them hoist the carcass into the air and we tied the other end of the rope to the tree to keep the shark away from the pigs.

Then I sat down on a log and something told me I was ill. On my left hand the skin was gone from sliding down the liana to escape the warrior animal and my shoulders and the insides of my arms were raw from fighting the shark. Watery fluid the color of yellow begonias was trickling from my skin and dripping onto the ground.

The husband of my dead wife's sister sat down next to me. His wife remained standing, but according to custom she could talk to me as long as a relative was present.

"You are bleeding," Mbugo told me. "You are wounded."

"Yes," I agreed. "But it's not bad. It's not bad bleeding."

"It's not the bleeding of death," he declared. "Still, it's bleeding. Any bleeding is unhealthy."

Her husband had said it. Now she could say it.

"You are hurt! Your bleeding is not good."

"I suppose so," I told her.

Davey

"Camellia leaves stop bleeding. He needs some camellia leaves," Aala told her husband with a concerned note in her voice.

Mbugo gave her a look.

"What do you think?" she asked, hoping for his approval.

"He needs some camellia leaves for his wounds," he agreed.

I wanted to avoid rudeness and, as is our custom, I looked at her under lowered eyelids. She was a fine looking woman. She seemed always to be smiling and I liked her expression better than the sullen look of other women and to my mind she stood out among them like an orchid encircled by decay.

A slight sigh escaped me.

"He must be in pain," she said indirectly.

"Thank you for letting your wife think of me," I told her husband.

He nodded.

I went on with my thoughts. Now I knew why I had never gazed at Aala like this before. Until the weakness which I felt today I had been strong enough to maintain the decision I had made not to admit that she bore a resemblance to her sister. Yet she was a nice looking woman. What beautiful breasts she had! They seemed like ripe fruits of her flesh in the same way that attractive flowers are part of their plants.

"Get some camellia leaves," Mbugo commanded.

"I will. And what about food? Do you think he is hungry?"

I was lost in thought. There was a rosy light on her skin and her nipples were slightly reddish like the red dots of lotuses growing on mountain lakes. Her skin was firm and smooth and with that rosy light on it and her smiling expression I thought her delightful and for a moment I forgot my discomfort.

"Are you hungry?" Mbugo demanded, irritated by what he perceived to be my slowness of response to an indirect question.

"Yes," I said. "But you asked a question. That is only an answer."

He frowned.

"You know something, Brother of Cloud in the Water? You are bleeding but your speech has not lost any blood."

"Does that disappoint you?" I asked him.

He stared at me with disapproval, but then he turned toward his wife.

"Get him some taro root," he commanded.

When she left I saw him looking at the shark.

"Half of that is yours," I said.

"Which half?"

"The tail. I am keeping the teeth."

"Good. The liver is in that half. The gills are worthless."

We sat in silence. It was difficult to talk to him. After a while I said, "I will give you the gills."

"Why?"

"Because you are poor."

"Poor! What do you mean poor?"

"Because taro is all you can offer. Taro root for a shark!"

"Poor!" he repeated. "Does a poor man have sago this far from the coast? I'll show you how poor I am. I'll have my wife bring you some sago. I will cut you a coconut myself."

"That is good. But if you need the gills say so. Does your wife have enough to eat?"

"Of course," he replied angrily. "But I'll tell you one thing. You spoiled her sister."

It was an old bone of contention and I was not going to gnaw on it now.

"And you're the strongest warrior!" he stated.

I waited. I heard the reproach in his voice.

"And the best hunter!" he continued.

"But what?" I demanded.

"But you're weak on women."

I knew he disliked me and I knew the reason. His wife liked me. She liked the way I had treated her sister. Now I turned to look at him and as I did so I remembered what it was that struck me whenever I saw him. It was his stern expression. His lips were set in a grim line and his broad nose with its wide nostrils which seemed always to flare in disapproval of anything excellent indicated even more than his eyes the limited extent of his understanding. He was very muscular and his huge forearms were as large as the calf muscles on the legs of most men. Above his severe lips and large nose his eyes were dull and lightless and his brows always set in a frown made his face look as though the world itself had served only to narrow his outlook and increase his dislike of what he saw.

Like most of us who had shunned the uncomfortable gourds worn by other tribes, he wore a loincloth and this one was covered by a purple strip of paper bark pounded from a mulberry tree. A cockatoo feather rose from his headdress of poison sea shells and when he turned his head the stem moved slightly but the yellow feather on the end of the stem waved gracefully in a wide arc. But I was looking at something else. A long time ago the tails of pigs had been suspended from his ears. That was because he had been a widower looking for a wife. He had killed his first wife for adultery.

"Why are you looking at my ears?" he asked.

"No reason," I said.

But he guessed the reason.

"You should wear the tails of pigs also," he told me. "You are a widower."

"But I am not a widower looking for a wife," I said sharply.

He was silent for only a moment and then he exclaimed, "Of course not! You were always the good husband," he indicated with a sneer.

"I hope so. But you sound as though I had caused you a problem."

The subject was distasteful and although I had turned away I was conscious of his watching me with his usual mixture of wonderment and annoyance.

"Why don't you let your beard grow? Or paint the special charcoal lines filled with red pigment about your eyes and mouth? That will show everybody you're not looking for a wife."

"If I looked it would be in spirit," I said. "Not in the flesh."

He had no answer. This time he stared at the shark. "Is that meat any good?"

"It is good if you need it. If you don't, I will kill you a tree kangaroo."

"Yes. That is proper considering the food I have given you."

"The food you will give me. Your food's in the future."
"But soon it will be here. Then it will be in the present."
"True. But I can't hunt until my hand and arms heal."
"I know that. I will wait. I can wait a long time for a tree kangaroo." And to show me he had a soul as lofty as a cloud he added, "Kill it when you feel well enough. Only when you feel well enough."
"You can count on it."
"I know that, Brother."
He stood up and looked down at me.
"I will have my wife take the food to the long house. When she boils the camellia leaves I will bring them to the long house myself."
"I will expect them, then."
"Certainly," he said and started to walk away. But something stopped him and I saw him turn around with another look of wonderment upon his face and this time it was not accompanied by irritation. He looked at my hair and then he touched the cockatoo feather he was wearing. It signified he had killed a man and I knew he was proud of it.
"You can wear thirty-two of these. Why don't you?"
"One is more beautiful," I told him.
He stood there thinking. Suddenly a smile appeared on his face and he nodded in agreement.
"That is true," he said and walked off.
I got up slowly and made my way to the long house and carefully lay down. I was too ill to answer questions and I went to sleep. But after a while I felt someone shaking me and I woke up.
"Your food is outside. Shall I get it?" Oranooa the old warrior asked.
"No," I said. "I will get it."
I managed to stand up and walk outside to retrieve a coconut and two clay pots and then carry them back into the long house. It seemed to take all my remaining strength just to sit down again and try to eat. The men moved near me but they were polite and even though they were curious no one asked me a question. My wife's sister had mixed the taro root with crab and I slowly finished the

Davey

taro root in one of the pots and then, after taking a deep breath, I ate the sweet potato from another and sipped the milk from the coconut before my eyelids felt so heavy that once more I could not stay awake.

8

A fire was burning when I awakened from the Sleeping World and the smoke was keeping the flies from landing on the rims of the pots. The men sat around me and the warmth of the fire and the warmth of their bodies and the smell of the tobacco they were smoking made me feel as though I had been on a dangerous journey from which I had returned without the strength I had had when I left. They spoke in low tones so as not to disturb me and I appreciated their courtesy. But I asked myself whether a warrior should be so exhausted. I was more exhausted than I had been after...

"Remember?" I heard a voice say.

"What?" a young warrior asked. His head net was unadorned and he was looking straight at me.

So the first voice must have been mine, I told myself. Had I been thinking of exhaustion after a battle?

"Remember our battle with the enemy tribe?" I continued vaguely.

"Which one? We have had many battles."

"True," I responded and tried to recall. Was it the one when we had surprised them at their ritual fornication after a cannibal feast? I asked myself. That time my feet had been wet with blood after I killed two people with one spear thrust, but I had not been exhausted. It must have been after some other battle and not after a raid, for a raid is not a battle. "Remember the battle I named after an Orchid Spider?" I said aloud.

"Yes. But you call it that. We call it the Battle of the Heads of Whores."

I nodded in agreement. The object had been to ambush the warriors and then to kill their women.

Suddenly I thought of how tired I'd been that day. It was odd, though. I felt more tired now. For during that battle I had suffered only from a strange sort of moral fatigue. Our tribe believes in one marriage and though we accept divorce, we punish adultery by death. Even personal relations with a distant relative is frowned upon. But prostitution is the religion of our enemy tribe and each warrior has several wives. To fulfill their duties they sell the sexual favors of their wives to any man who has an extra pig or spear or even two taro roots. Fathers sell their wives to their own sons and the skin of the men and women so honored is scarified by sacred designs.

It had been a depressing battle because after ambushing the warriors we had killed many of their women. But a man is no more than his history. I wanted to keep the record straight.

"I set the ambush, if you recall. We were like the camouflaged spider hiding inside the orchid and they were the unsuspecting moth. That's why I call it the Battle of the Orchid Spider. I planned it that way. But we are headhunters, so if you want to say *heads* I must say Heads of Warriors."

"Yes," he reluctantly agreed. "You yourself killed only men." He pointed behind me. "Your six are back there."

An unexpected curiosity overcame me and despite my fatigue I stood up slowly and walked toward the back of the long house. On a shelf of black palm wood raised high above the floor in the place of sacrificial honor my own thirty-two skulls were arranged in a line with six set apart from the others. As I looked at them I told myself that the husband of my wife's sister had been wrong about the thirty-two cockatoo feathers. I could wear thirty-eight.

Jumping spiders were living in the brain pans of the skulls and they had woven webs of gray silk in the eye sockets of the skulls and threads of gray led into the brain area between the bone and the back teeth. Suddenly a ray of sunlight on the roof filtered through the thatch and then the webs became white and the threads seemed almost to glisten. An adult male spider which had just molted was iridescently black in the light while on his legs little tufts of fuzz appeared duller until he moved away. But it irritated me to see these spiders taking over my skulls. I had forgotten that it is dangerous to give anything a definitive name and when I had spoken out loud obviously the spiders had been listening. They were not orchid spiders but I knew that made no difference for they belonged to the spider tribe and now they were sharing success with their orchid totem. I did not disturb them. For I wondered if their webs were ears and whether speech sent them messages through touch and then I told myself that spiders understood that every man has ghosts. He is haunted by the words he has spoken.

Now my own words came back to me. I remembered every one. I could not forget the speech with which I had planned our most successful battle.

"Warriors," I had said, "when I was a child I was deep in the forest watching a beautiful orchid. It was twilight and moths were beginning to fly. But there was enough light so that I could still see color and I was fascinated by the greenish yellow leaves of the orchid, twisting in spirals but growing straight upward. Under them two petals the size of a man's thumb grew level with the ground and they were white but tinged with pink like streaks of blood left on some tiny salt flat near the Lake of the World. Under them a single leaf hung down and it too was white but running through it I saw veins that looked as though they were actually bleeding. Then from the dim forest in front of me a black and orange moth flew toward the orchid and noiselessly circled around it. In the fading light the orchid seemed almost to glow in the dark and I sensed that the orchid attracted the moth by the light shining through darkness with its pale promise of beauty and nectar. The moth lit inside the orchid and for an instant the frail orchid shook under the weight of his landing. But suddenly I saw his body turned violently upside down and I found myself looking at the black and orange stripes of his belly. For inside the orchid, the same greenish yellow color as the petals themselves, an orchid spider had seized the moth and as I watched the ambush the wings of the moth ceased to beat."

I paused but after a short pause someone asked me, "Why are you telling us this?"

Davey

"Because I knew then that if you have to kill people this is the way to do it."

A long silence followed. Then one of the old men demanded, "And what orchid attracts the enemy?"

"Women," I replied quietly.

We had been in the long house talking in low tones as indeed we had been today. Yet the word had almost echoed from the walls. The last word seemed to suffocate us. We sat there appalled by the thoughts that my words suggested.

"Whose women?"

"Not their own. They are used to those."

Our thoughts became worse and we remained without speaking, gripped by a hush that was also intolerable.

Then I remembered something else. "We are outnumbered," the old man had remarked in order to state the fact and break the silence.

"Badly outnumbered," someone added, emphasizing the word *badly*.

"Naturally," I agreed. "Many wives have many children. This is nothing new to us. Prostitution has its advantages."

"Are you recommending it?" another warrior challenged me. As he spoke the curled boar's tusks he wore in his nostrils were gleaming in the gloom of the house.

"Don't answer that," the old man advised me.

Then they all turned on the warrior who had never taken a head and who had no notches on his spears.

"You are stupid!"

"You were born with a caul!"

"You ought to have been buried alive, not your twin brother!"

"Tell him. Tell him your words were not good."

"I have never told any man that," the warrior shouted.

They all grabbed their spears. Old and young there were twenty of them and they formed a circle around him.

"Don't you know he's our Chief!" they exclaimed.

"We have no Chief. You told us that. You said so yourselves," he retorted.

But they were angry and they cared not at all if secrets escaped.

"Fool! Don't you know why we say that? We have always been outnumbered. Have you thought of that? Do you know by how much? By twelve to one!"

"And what difference does that make? If you were younger and stronger you would look forward to killing many enemies."

"Idiot! Do you have ears? Are they connected to your brain?"

The warrior jumped to his feet.

"You call me a fool once more and I will kill you, ancient one," he shouted, singling out the oldest man.

"A fool can threaten. But can he understand?"

"Let him try," another warrior interrupted, trying to diffuse the situation. "Maybe he will pay attention to me. He is so vain he is not listening to you." He faced him directly. "Look at it this way," he began. "If they knew we had a Chief, they would know who did the planning. They would not rest until they killed him. With false information they are kept in doubt. They know where the body is but they cannot locate the head."

There was another silence. The first warrior finally looked at me.

"My words were not good," he admitted at last.

"They are good now," I said. But everyone knew that the argument had been an interruption more welcome than discussing the main subject.

Outside the long house dogs began barking and the noise interrupted these memories. I sat down again on a mat of palm fronds and tried to resume my thoughts but suddenly a new dog added his voice to the barking and the sound was answered by the squealing of pigs. Slowly I became aware that I was frowning. I lifted my head and again when I looked at the line of skulls I knew it was only the last six I was studying. Once they had been living warriors participating in a rape. Now spider webs and sprays of dried orchids lay around them, browned with smoke, brittle and unattractive. I decided I would have to find new orchids with which to adorn them. It would not be easy. They grew deep in the forest and I would have to take care not to harm the spiders lurking inside them.

Then the sound of voices came back to me in my memory and

unfortunately what I had previously said also returned.

"Whose women?" someone repeated.

"Ours," I had said bluntly.

"Won't one woman do?"

I shook my head. "Have you heard those sacred drums they carry?" I asked.

"You didn't answer my question!"

"I answered, but you didn't listen. Now you haven't answered mine. Have you heard those drums?" I repeated.

"Of course. We all have. What has that got to do—"

"I'll tell you. It has got to do with sound. They beat those drums when they find a virgin to deflower."

"Everyone knows that. Even I know that," he said in a haughty manner.

"Then if you know that, have you thought what would happen if they found two virgins in the forest?"

"No."

"Well, I have. I have had to think of that. I can almost hear it. The forest would ring with whoops. Then the sound of drums would reach their village. The place of deflowerment would fill with young men."

"And warriors," someone added.

"And warriors," I agreed. "But our own warriors would already be there, and their bodies would be covered by clay mixed with moss. Even our spears and our bows and arrows would be colored green. We would conceal ourselves in the green knife grass and when many of their warriors arrived, then we would ambush them like—"

"Like an orchid spider!"

"They would become like the moth of my childhood," I concluded.

Then the old men had held a council and the warriors went away and held a council of their own. At last everyone returned.

"It is an evil and wonderful plan, they all agreed."

"Your words describe it," I said.

"It is brilliant. It is worthy of a Chief."

"It is unworthy of a man," I commented.

"You are not a man. A man is anybody. You are somebody."
"Somebody who has the responsibility for terror," I told them.
"Yes. And it is a terror for a tribe to cease living."
"And it is terrible to use innocence simply to survive."
"We know that, Brother of Cloud in the Water. But a tribe must survive. A tribe must continue."
"So which is worse?" I asked.
"For a tribe to die," another elder insisted.
He stood up. He had an air of authority and I knew he had been a great battle chief. Against the white hairs on his chest a ceremonial necklace of beetles strung for each victory glinted in the firelight, polished with pig fat to keep them brilliantly green.
"Brother of Cloud in the Water, there is one thing you have not considered."
"I am willing to hear it."
"You won't like it."
"I will say so in that case."
"Good. Sometimes it is good to listen."
"I am listening. But there are no words to hear."
"You will hear them when they tell you this. We are not threatened by warriors alone. We are threatened also by their women."
I stood there, thinking. Then I held out my arm.
"Do you see an arrow scar there?"
"Yes. It has healed, but I see it."
"Then who do you think shot the arrow?" I asked. "A woman?"
But I knew he was clever and as I sometimes did, he answered by asking a question.
"Who has more scars? You or me?"
"I do," I said.
"And you are younger. Much younger. But I was a fight leader, so why do I have fewer scars?"
"I don't know the answer, unless you have more spirits on your side."
"I'll tell you the answer. I had fewer enemies. You have many more. Now why is that?"
Suddenly I knew he was right. Not only had the numbers of our

enemies increased, but greatly increased. They had taken to massing in groups and with the use of spotters they would loose thick flights of arrows at us and, using the wind, their arrows would tear through the kunai grass and come down as closely together as hailstones did on the distant mountains. For the first time we had started to carry large shields.

"So what are you saying?"

"I am saying that we are threatened by their women. The warriors may begin the process, but the women are having the children."

"And children grow into warriors," the first elder agreed.

I was silent. I waited for the fight leader to continue.

"Your plan is excellent," he told me. "But it has only one part."

"And you want a second part?" I asked.

"Yes. It is necessary."

I glanced at him coldly.

"And the second part is for men to make war on women?"

"On whores!" he exclaimed. "Not on women. On whores."

"I see. In their tribe there's a difference, is there?"

Angry shouts answered me.

"What's wrong with you? Of course there is."

"He's fallen in love with evil. I told you! I told you so."

"Brother of Cloud in the Water—"

"That's not my name. You have made a mistake. Now you want me to be the Warrior Who Makes War on Women."

"Brother of Cloud in the Water—"

I was staring straight through him as though he did not exist.

"Listen to me. We need their heads."

"The heads of whores!" a young warrior cried gleefully.

"Listen to me," the fight leader continued. "I have done the counting. We must have at least thirty heads to control their future offspring."

An excited voice rose once again in our midst. "Thirty whores' heads! The heads of thirty whores!"

"Who is that fool? Make him stand up," I commanded.

I watched him rising reluctantly and as I studied his body standing there with his lower lip jutting out and his small and shifty eyes seeking some place to look other than at me, my thoughts told me that our youth wasn't as it used to be and also that he was crestfallen and ashamed of the figure he had cut in front of the old men and the warriors. I wanted to make his embarrassment worse so that perhaps he would learn to keep his inexperienced emotions in check.

"Do you know your name?" I demanded.

"Of course."

"So that's one thing you know. Do you know a second? Maybe you know that death is a joke. Is it?"

"No," he answered, but I wondered if he believed it.

"I will tell you a third. We are headhunters. We do not keep skulls which are jokes."

Then I told him to sit down and I turned back to the old battle chief.

"Listen! I have already disgraced myself by proposing two women as bait for an ambush. I will not kill any more."

"You won't have to," he replied. "Divide your force. Let the first force kill the warriors. Stay with them. Then, after the ambush, send the second force to kill the women. But be sure, now, that they bring back the heads."

It alarmed me that he might be suggesting a necessity since behind my distaste for butchery I glimpsed the terrible shining of something half hidden, something as dim but as actual as starlight through clouds. He was proposing a barter. We would exchange thirty skulls for something intangible. Something called Time.

"I want a vote on this," I said.

They were shocked. We do not do things that way. Decisions were made and never voted on and responsibility was not a matter to be decided in common. But I insisted and I told them to make two circles of skulls taken by our ancestors. The skulls were so old they were without their jaws and they were the color of smoke and covered with dust. All of them were fragile and as a warrior placed one of them in a circle the front teeth fell out.

"Can I keep these?" he asked, after having collected them in the palm of his hand.

Immediately an old man with feathers past their prime arranged

Davey

in his head net answered him harshly.
"No! We know what you want to do. You want to make a necklace, don't you?"
The warrior nodded.
"Use dogs' teeth! You are a good warrior, but you did not take this skull. My grandfather did, so it is for me to say!" He held out his arm with his cupped palm held upward. "Give them to me. I will have the wood carver fit them into the sacred drum."
The rest of the men were gazing at me with a sense of curiosity concerning what I was about to do. I waited a moment and then I held my hand over one of the circles and took my knife of cassowary bone and cut my left wrist. My blood gushed into the circle and after the circle was entirely red I squeezed my wrist above the veins with my other hand and then the blood dripped more slowly. I wanted to show my tribe that what the old warrior had proposed was something deadly serious and by looking at their faces I saw I had succeeded.
"The circle with the blood says we will slaughter thirty enemy women. The circle without the blood says we will not do so. We will do what the stones say."
Then I told each man to go outside and pick up a pebble and when he came back to place the pebble inside one of the circles. I myself picked up a white pebble but as I did so I had to let go of my wrist and my blood started dripping over the ground. Looking around I quickly found a small creeper to tie tightly around my wrist and by the time I walked inside the long house with the other men the bleeding had once again slowed.
I myself placed a stone and I stood there as a large number of men crowded forward to place the stones in the skull circles. It seemed to take a long time but when they were through I saw that all the stones except one were in the circle which I had wet with my blood. My lone white pebble I had placed in the dry one.
Everyone sat down but I remained standing to address them.
"All right," I concluded. "We will slaughter the enemy women."
But there is always someone with a fine taste for language.
"Why do you say *slaughter*? That is a word we use for pigs."

Brother of Cloud in the Water

The whole thing made me angry. To begin with it had not been my plan. Using the intrigue of the Orchid Spider to ambush the worthy opponent warriors was now being overshadowed by an additional scheme to slaughter unarmed women. I would have to delegate authority for the second part of the plan and I still believed that that part was beneath the dignity of a warrior.

With great restraint I did not shout the answer to the previous question but I turned a cold eye on the man. He was someone I had never liked.

"I say *slaughter* because that is the word I wish to say. You do not slaughter warriors. You cannot be that lucky. Warriors can defend themselves. But what do you expect women to do? Defend themselves with their digging sticks?"

Insensitive as he was, he did not read my expression and repeated his argument.

"You should say *kill*. *Slaughter* is used for animals."

Stupid people need obvious actions. I walked up to him and stared him in his face.

"I will say *slaughter* because the word is exact. I will say *slaughter* unless you plan to prevent me."

There was silence. I stood there another moment and then I turned and walked back to the other side of the circle. I described the details of my own plan and then I delegated the second part to another. When we were through going over the ambush I added one last requirement.

"There's another condition."

"Another condition!"

"Yes. It must be understood that I am not to blame for whatever girls must be chosen. Is that understood?"

They nodded.

"All right. But don't forget. My fight is with warriors only."

"Yes," they said with one voice.

Now I took a last look at the skulls of the six warriors I had killed on the day of the ambush and as I did so a gust of wind stirred some loose palm fronds on the roof and the white and glistening spider webs made me realize that I should not be too proud of the success

Davey

of my ambush. A spider had thought of it first.

9

I went back and lay down near the pots of food belonging to my wife's sister. Squatting near them and holding a brindle piglet in his arms, a friend of mine was smiling. I knew he had seen me staring at the skulls of the six warriors and then I sensed that in my weariness I had unconsciously spent a long time to do so.

He nodded toward the skulls. "You have many things to take care of," he told me.

Saseve was a good man and his pleasant look managed to soften the impression of his fierce black beard. Under his long nose with its upturned end that seemed to suggest amusement, his teeth were somehow white despite all the smoking he did. He was known for his love of pigs and fairness in his family. Coiled beside him one end of a small grass rope was tied to a post and the other end was fastened to the foot of his piglet.

He lifted the piglet with one hand on either side of its ribcage and when he placed it carefully upon the floor it immediately trotted over toward my food. But my friend pulled back on the rope without jerking it and the jovial little animal, after making a few more tries in the direction of the food and then seeing it could not get what it wanted, finally walked backed toward its owner and, standing on its hind legs, put its front feet in his lap. He picked it up again and stroked automatically with the manner of a man who was thinking something else. Saseve was not smiling any more.

"That was a bad day," he stated.

"It was even more dangerous than we could have thought," I agreed. We had been together during the ambush.

Davey

"Do you remember the Woman with Hair the Color of Blood?" he asked.

"How could I forget? She almost got every warrior killed."

My mind raced back to the day before the battle. Just after the previous evening rains had stopped and the morning mists were beginning to release their grip from the lower mountains and the afternoon spirits were beginning to move, a now familiar but rare sound began to reach my ears. I couldn't believe I was hearing it once more. As with many things in life I had wished for, there had always been hope but never a certainty. When the noise like a large swarm of bees became louder I hurried out into the open area near our older gardens where we had laboriously cleared a landing path and I looked up into the sky. Everyone in the tribe had seen me rushing down between the huts and leaping over the perimeter wall. First the children followed with shouts and then their parents became so excited that even the adults were jumping up and down with delight.

"Is that a Bird of Ghosts!" they exclaimed? "A *second* Bird of Ghosts?"

"I told you it would come!" I exclaimed, relieved to be justified at last.

"We hear it! We hear it!"

"You doubted me. Now, once more, you see I tell the truth!"

Without replying or apologizing for their skepticism, everyone continued shouting. "We will have more brown food and sweet sand that melts in the mouth!"

"And more magic axes!"

"We see it! We see it!"

"Here it comes!"

Out of the fog appeared a bird smaller than the first one, but this time with a regular rhythmic noise coming from its throat. Lower and lower it came. Then, on the sunlight side of its body a magic hole appeared, darker than the rest of its feathers. I knew we must be seeing another special spirit and just like the first Bird I told you about, Forest Spring, again I could hardly contain my joy. Once again our tribe was to be blessed by a mighty Ancestor in the Sky.

He must have seen all our work to make him more comfortable on the newly cleared ground and was going to accept our invitation to land.

My heart started to pound with anticipation. I waited for the Bird to set its wings and not to crash through the treetops as the first Bird of Ghosts had done, but to come easily onto its flat nesting spot.

However, it remained aloft. Perhaps our actions were frightening it.

Instead, out of its side and not out of its bottom floated two large white mushrooms with long ropes attached to something below them and looking almost like the hooded jellyfish that live in the Lake of the World and which glide through the water with their long poisonous tendrils floating along beneath. This I should have known was an omen, but I was so excited that I disregarded my instincts.

Circling, this Bird ignored its beautiful landing area, and, as it continued on its skyward journey to gain height with each minute, it did not seem wounded by the loss of the mushrooms. In fact, it jauntily tipped its wings while almost simultaneously with its disappearance back into the clouds the two white mushrooms floated down from above.

Little by little the objects got lower in the sky.

Disappointed by its departure, but still excited, the people shouted, "The Bird must be sending us gifts!"

But suddenly there were shrieks of a different kind.

As soon as the women and children saw that a sacrificial warrior was attached to the bottom of one of the mushrooms, they screamed in terror, leaped back over the garden walls, and ran inside their houses, making sure to pull their thatched door covers behind them. The joy of a few minutes earlier now became a worry and I directed several of our tribesmen to hurry and retrieve spears for those who had left them behind.

Over the treetops the mushrooms plunged. First a large square box made of some woven vines bumped heavily to the ground. Soon afterward the second mushroom deposited the sacrifice near it with a thump. We waited a few moments in silence and then carefully we inched closer to look down at the strange warrior. Instantly we jumped back. He was not dead as we had expected. He was very much alive.

It was truly magical. Even the mushrooms had softened in flight, lost their gills, and turned into some kind of smooth material that kept moving slightly like leaves with each new breeze even when they were on the ground.

We circled him. Raising their spears some of the men shouted loud warnings and many of them ran at him with threatening gestures. But I began to worry that we might be offending the distant Spirit which had allowed him to come here and finally I persuaded the men to retreat for a moment to see what would happen.

The live sacrifice was very strange. He did not spring to his feet like a warrior. From a sitting position he rolled over to a kneeling position. Then he pushed himself upright with the aid of his arms. He was wearing some sort of armored clothing that covered him all over, not unlike the skins on the chests of the sacrifices in the first Bird. Even laced skins covered his lower legs. This person also wore a headdress of thin brown skin with ear flaps hanging down on each side of his cheeks and we could not see his face because of clear growths bulging out in front of each of his eyes.

The magic continued to happen. Not only was he able to pull off his headdress and eye coverings as easily as a snake sheds its old skin but by the time he had untied himself from the mushrooms he had instantly changed himself from a warrior into a Woman With Hair the Color of Blood.

Some of the men again raised their spears, but she stood her ground and smiled. Showing no fear whatsoever, she put her hand inside one of her pockets, but before she could withdraw it, one of our younger warriors with no patience thought she had a weapon and he threw a wild spear at her which she calmly sidestepped. Then she stood her ground again. Lowering their spears the other warriors laughed and chided him.

"You couldn't defend us if you had to!"

"Even a woman is safe from you in the same forest. How are you

going to kill any whores tomorrow?"
"Go back to your hut and practice!"
Ashamed and resentful, he slunk off, muttering to himself.
Removing her hand from her clothing, she offered us what looked like stick tobacco. At first no one moved. Then one man tentatively extended his hand towards hers and after a quick retreat he showed the offering to his friends. Soon others also creeped cautiously forward to accept her gifts. She began speaking some words to them that I did not understand and I whispered to a friend.
"Go find the Maker of Language...," I began to say when she interrupted me. I was startled.
"An interpreter won't be necessary," she said, this time in our own language. "I must have landed so hard it shook your dialect from my mind. I am familiar with your tribe."
This was double magic and I was the only one brave enough to speak.
"That may be," I replied, as I stood straighter. "We are the People of the Only World. Not only that, but today you have proven that history can repeat itself."
"How it that?" she inquired.
"In the long ago our ancestors told us about a Woman Who Came Down from the Sky. You have arrived the same way."
"Oh! You mean Kau. I have not heard her story in a long time."
"Then I will remind everyone," I said.
"On a warm day when food would spoil quickly, a tribesman was eating the raw flesh of a small fish as he sat on the edge of a stream. Suddenly he saw a woman coming down from the sky and when she was standing in front of him, he was afraid. She asked him why he had not cooked his fish. He did not know what she was talking about but he thought he might have offended her when she refused his offering to join him.
A warrior cannot admit his ignorance on anything, especially to a woman, so he was not pleased when she ordered him to cook sago and coconuts as well as the fish. He had never experienced such things. But, because she was an Old Spirit, the sky woman understood his ignorance and offered to remain as his wife. He

agreed only out of fear. She showed him what fire was and how to prepare food in the correct manner, the way we do this today.

But the warrior was not happy with the arrangement. He had a wife in the village to do womans' work and when Kau saw that she was not wanted, she went back up to the sky once more and never returned. Embarrassed by the events, the warrior buried the extra sago and coconuts which she had brought so that his tribe would not question him. But the fire was too obvious to be extinguished and the plants refused to hide. Eventually they sprouted and grew and over time the story of the sky woman became known."

"You are a good story teller," she complimented me. "Stories are important to keep history alive." While holding her hands in front of her at waist level she started lifting her elbows a little and moving her arms up and down like small fledglings do with their wings when their parents return to the nest. "Oh, I am so excited to be here!"

"Who are you?" I inquired. "Do you live in the sky?"

"I am an ethnologist," she answered with another smile, and I could see that she was scrutinizing all of us but me in particular, especially my straight hair and long nose.

I stared back at her. "What does that word mean?" I asked.

"Oh, it just means that I study tribes. Your tribe especially."

"How can you study what you do not know exists? You have not been here before."

"But I have been told so much about you! And I study ancient tribes as well as present ones."

"That would mean that some tribes have not survived," I said, and looked meaningfully at the other men. Everyone knew I was talking about the raid we had just planned. And here it was being justified by an outsider who came from Another World.

"Are there any elders here?" she asked hopefully.

I was suspicious of such a question. Perhaps she had the power to harm them. "Why do you ask?"

"They would remember a white man with red hair visiting this village before you and I were born."

I turned and looked at Oranooa, the oldest warrior, with the question on my face. He thought for what seemed to be a long time.

Then he nodded.

"Yes, it is true," he agreed. "He was the first white man to live among us. The Madman on the River was the second. You will be the third in our memory."

"Oh, we will have so much to talk about!" She slowed down for only a second. "With your permission, of course," she said jovially. "I must not forget my manners."

I was relieved that this sky woman was seemingly speaking some truth and not filling the minds of the young men with mysterious thoughts.

"How do you know of this?" I asked.

"That man was my father."

"What did he name you?"

"Arana. Arana Smyth."

"He named you after this island," Oranooa said to her.

"Yes," she agreed. "After New Aran Island." She looked directly at me. "And what is your name?" she inquired.

I had started to admire her bravery in a new land and I replied, "Manosoma, but my people call me Brother of Cloud in the Water."

"What an interesting name! Tribes of American Indians have excellent names also. Story names like Swift Water, Half Moon, Broken Arrow and Running Horse."

"What is a horse?" I asked. "And where are these people? They are not on this island."

She had heard my irritation and stated, "You do not need to worry."

"I am not worried."

"They are far, far away. Even farther away than my island home in England."

Now I really doubted her.

"Are these islands in the sky or on the Lake of the World?" I asked.

"Some things are real even if we cannot see them," she replied. "Is not the moon still in the sky even when she sleeps and you cannot see her?"

Davey

I nodded in agreement. "With the moon, this is true."

"Then understand that there are faraway islands on the Lake of the World that are too distant to see and that are no threat to your people," she said calmly.

"Distance is one truth," I told her. "Danger is yet another."

The sun was now directly above us on his daily path to meet with the ocean later in the afternoon and his rays were baking the earth on which we stood.

"Truth is an interesting topic to talk about," she answered as she wiped the perspiration from her forehead.

Discussing such topics with a stranger, particularly a woman stranger, struck me as being very odd, and I wanted to think this over before continuing. "Perhaps you would like to sit in the shade," I suggested.

"That would be wonderful," she agreed, and, with her direction, the men opened her large box and carried smaller boxes up to the village and placed them inside my hut.

I walked through the grass curtain covering the door and the Woman With Hair the Color of Blood followed me inside.

"You may stay here while you visit. My wife will not object."

"Has she gone to see her parents?" the sky woman inquired, seemingly familiar with some of our customs.

"In a way, yes. She is with her mother in the Spirit World."

For some reason the woman's eyes instantly welled up with tears and she said, "You must miss her terribly. I am so sorry."

"Don't be sorry. Kindred spirits are never far apart." Wishing to change the subject I inquired, "How is it that you are alone on this journey?"

She sighed. "There is no one to care anymore. I have no family. They are all dead, or might as well be."

"Killed in battle?" I asked.

"No. Just dead. Except for my ex-husband."

"And he isn't still concerned?"

She gave a hard laugh. "This missionary is only concerned for his reputation in gathering a larger 'flock' than other missionaries," she retorted and then added, "but I realize you have never seen an animal

called a sheep, so think of it like a group of birds all together."
"Being anxious for one's tribe is quite normal," I commented.
"His flock is not his tribe," she quickly retorted bitterly. "Do you know what he said to me only a few weeks ago on the beach near Port Moresby?"
"I would have no idea."
"It was partly on the subject of truth, oddly enough." He said to me, "I'm proud to be a missionary. And I remember your rotten definition."
"What was that?" I replied. "It was probably specific to you alone."
"You mean you've forgotten?"
"Well, I have other things to think of, Cedric."
"I know. Things like circumcision of virgin girls and whether Bedouins use their left hands for bodily functions. High-minded things."
"Thank you. But you're high-minded enough for both of us."
"I couldn't agree more. Your definition of a missionary was definitely low-minded."
"I'm sorry if it hurt your feelings, Cedric."
"Think nothing of it. A missionary is used to savage misunderstanding."
"Listen to that. Ethnology still angers you, doesn't it?"
"Only when it defines truth in terms of doubt."
"Truth! There you go again. What in the world did I say?"
She told me that he had raised his head in a gesture of recollection while his eyes gazed without focusing at the horizon of sea and sky.
"You said, 'You have turned your training into the pride of humility, the selfishness of selflessness, and the art of gaining international benefits of nationalism while appearing to do things for the disadvantaged.'"
"I said that?"
"You did."
"Well, thanks for reminding me. I didn't know I could put things that well."
"You are as bad as Flaubert. You love the bizarre and the

barbarous."

She recalled that her eyes had flashed and that she had made an impatient gesture. "You must have always hated my plain language. I say undertaker. I don't say mortician. Oh! I must not forget."

And she told me that she had given him a malicious look.

"I must not forget that while I am talking you are not listening and you are probably thinking of God and since God is thought thinking thought your thinking is a thinking on thinking."

"Arana, when are you going to stop bringing that up? I'm getting sick of it. Saint Thomas is rather distinguished, after all."

"And so is wrestling an alligator. The Seminoles do similar feats in the States."

I was not familiar with the names and references she was using, but apparently their disagreement had been interrupted by a hand tapping her soon-to-be ex-husband on the shoulder and a voice asking him in Pidgin English, "Bringum smoke smoke fire long boy?"

"What's that savage want, Arana? Just look at him. He's wearing a necklace of human teeth."

"Yes. That's interesting. They're all incisors. Must have taken quite a few skulls to make a necklace like that."

"Well, what's he want?"

"Don't you know, dear?"

"Of course I don't know. Tell me what he wants."

"Oh. He wants a light, Cedric."

A soft noise above her head brought her back to the present. When she glanced upward I could see her looking at a small python coiled round a rafter. About twelve inches of its body was extended out towards her and its triangular head was gazing directly at her while its flicking tongue moved in and out of its square snout.

"Um.... Do you think you could put the snake back out in the forest?" she asked me, as she slowly backed away.

I smiled. "That is my house snake," I explained, "to keep the rats away. She's just trying to find out who you are."

"Even I don't know the answer to that life question."

I didn't let her see that I liked her answer. "Well, just forget her.

She won't bother you."

The woman grimaced. "Are you sure?"

"Would you prefer the rats nibbling on you?"

She rolled her eyes and then said, "All right. I'll trust your judgment." Then her mind seemed unwilling to forget her missionary ex-husband and she inquired, "Do you think you could ever believe in only one god? I know your language does not have a term for this idea, but do you know what I mean?"

I was becoming more comfortable with her, so I replied, "Our mountain enemies believe in Harisu, the Supreme Being. He has the right to preside over all other Council Chiefs. This is not our way and our Ancestors do not agree with it for we believe in many Supreme Spirits. It would be an insult to name them as one. The Sea Spirit would cause all the fish to swim away, the Sky Spirit would throw stars at the land, the Earth Spirit would roll burning rocks down upon us, and the Wind Spirits would blow us from our homes."

"That is fascinating!" she announced with her smile once more on her face. "It's just what I thought you'd say. My father was never able to make contact with your enemies in his research. And it pleases me that you would not give in to Cedric's absurd notion that all cultures should think and believe as one."

Tribesmen were still milling about the front of my hut and sticking their heads in from time to time to see if the sky woman had opened her boxes. Each man knew that he would gain in stature with his wife if he were the first to obtain the sweet brown food and to tell her what other mysteries the boxes held. Repeatedly I told them it was getting late and that they must prepare for tomorrow's fighting, but, as usual, like over-excited children they were too wound-up to listen.

"Keep away", I finally warned them. "We will find the magic in the boxes after tomorrow. But right now I am putting a tonog on this place. He will kill you. He is the ghost of a ghost."

Instantly they hurried away, muttering among themselves. "We must go. That is the worst thing there is."

10

After I had put the screen of rushes in front of the door, I saw Arana looking at me.

"You invented the tonogs, didn't you?" she asked me.

"Yes," I said. "With fools you have to be foolish."

She gave me a look of understanding and then immediately busied herself, as women seem compelled to do, with little tasks of organization. As she did this I moved two skulls off my bed of bark, placed them along the wall, and sat down to watch her.

First she took what looked like a large net bag from one of her boxes. Unlike our head nets, this one had a rope attached onto each end and she proceeded to tie it crosswise in a corner so that it was suspended about three feet off the floor.

"What is the purpose of that?" I inquired.

"It's my bed. It is called a hammock."

"You don't sleep on the ground with a skull as a pillow?"

She shook her head and handed me a small square object that was very soft to the touch. "That is my pillow. It is filled with bird feathers."

"And is that your virginal bed?"

She laughed almost to hysteria. "Good heavens, no! I never thought of it that way. What made you say that?"

"It doesn't look as if it would suit a couple."

"Oh, my. Men's thoughts are universally the same, no doubt about it. Would you like to try it in spite of your notions? Men use them also."

"No," I replied. "There are many good reasons to sleep on the ground."

"You mean other than to be with a woman?"

"Of course."

"What are they?"

"You can feel the approach of someone as their feet shake the earth. And if it's an enemy who has gotten past the sentries, it would be more difficult for that person to spear a man who is sleeping flat on the floor than it would be to hit someone suspended in the air."

"Well, so much for luxury. Don't you want to relax once in a while?"

"A warrior needs to stay strong, to be hardened, and your hammock would only soften him."

"Then let me see how your bark bed feels," she said as she sat down beside me.

She settled into its surface and looked pleasantly surprised. "Not bad. It's fluffier than it looks. You do like a tiny bit of comfort."

Smoke was rising from the small fire in the middle of the hut and we heard a brief afternoon shower dripping off the tips of rushes around the edges.

"I would like to see you with your skin off," I told her.

"What?" she exclaimed, quickly leaning away from me in a tense manner.

"Those skins you wear beneath your knees."

"Oh, you mean my boots!"

"What did you think I meant?"

"Never mind," she replied, as she unlaced them, but she still had something on beneath the skins.

"And what are those?" I asked.

"Those are my riding breeches," she informed me, and I told her to take them off too.

She refused, but eyed me with a coy expression on her face, so I pulled them off the way you skin a snake and I sat there looking at her legs. There were magical markings like scars below her knees like two bones crossed one over the other but they faded and she was like everyone else.

She tossed her head and her flaming red hair moved to the side

Davey

and she herself took off the strange things she wore over her chest. But I have seen many women with never a surprise and like our young girls the sky woman's breasts were high and sticking out while her stomach was flat and not rounded. Then she leaned in towards me.

Eleven times we made one body together before the sun kissed the sea and when we ceased my arms ached when I pushed myself up and slowly I understood that my knees were bleeding where they had gone through the moss and into the sand.

For some reason she had begun to call me a god. "Oh, God, make love to me," she had yelled. "Oh, I want to die. I want to die with God." Later, she lay there as though dead but then I heard some words from her mouth as new as the breeze before storms and she started repeating, "Never... in all my life... never...." Suddenly she sat up and stared at me seriously.

"Did you feel them?" she asked.

And I nodded because I too had felt these waves without whitetops cresting and they had been moving from the land toward the sea.

That evening the warriors came up to me asking, "What happened? She was shrieking like pigs we slaughter. All afternoon she shrieked the way pigs do." They had no idea I had been one with her because our women are silent at these times so I was explaining, "A god visited her," as she happened past. Arana agreed and said in a strange voice, "Yes, I was visited by God."

Later, when they had left, I contradicted her.

"A 'God' did not visit you this afternoon. I did."

She looked at me in a way I have never seen on the faces of women in The Only World and she replied, "No. It was God. Don't you think I know God when I feel him?"

Despite the fact that I felt she was referring to a god in a different way than I might do, as a leader my People I am used to being considered a type of god or spirit due to my position and I decided, rather than to confront her, that I would continue to observe her and her strange ways.

I slept in the men's long house that night as we prepared for the

Battle of the Orchid Spider. It was a dark night and the wild spirits were everywhere. I had trouble getting the warriors to follow me with only the stars to guide us but I convinced them that this was a perfect start to a perfect ambush. We headed uphill through the trees. Wide expanses of tiger grass waved over our heads, almost obscuring the sky, and brushing our faces with their long tassels. After three hours of adjusting our path and using as many game trails as possible to save our strength we knew we were near the enemy and the warriors concealed themselves as planned, leaving only the two unfortunate virgins out in the open.

Then, just as my plan was working and we had almost everything to our advantage, there came an enraged yell at the enemy men attracted to our women, and I was stunned to see the Woman With Hair the Color of Blood rush in to intervene. She had apparently followed us to battle from a distance and our inexperienced warriors bringing up the rear had not heard her.

"Stop that!" she had shrieked. "Stop that right this instant!"

Above us gigantic trees were reaching to the sky and screeches of invisible excited birds were added to the chaos of the moment. Dropping out of the high branches, bits of broken vines and bark and bird droppings rained down on us as I fought off the enemy warriors trying to grab this new prize.

"Go away!" I shouted at her. "Get out of here!"

An enemy warrior and I fell on a mass of powerful twisted roots and I struggled in the tangled vines at the base of the trunks to keep my footing as I kept sliding on the dark brown decaying leaves. Time after time my warriors were overcome by the other tribe and yet we just managed to survive until we could withdraw with thirty of their heads.

On our way home a deafening roar of rain came down through the high canopy of leaves, covering our trail and running down the mountainside in swift rivulets. Furious as I was with the sky woman, when we reached the village I knew that something more than stupidity was wrong with her.

In the heat of the day she was shaking with cold.

"My nose feels hot," she told me. "And my back hurts."

Davey

"It probably happened when I wrenched you away from the grasp of the second warrior," I said in a non-sympathetic way.

She ignored my comment. "No, it's more than that. Even my eyeballs hurt when I move them. They feel like they are on rubber bands attached to the back of my skull."

Her words were confusing me again and I was worried that she had brought a bad spirit back with her from the enemy camp.

"I've got to lie down. I'm dizzy."

Slowly she eased herself into her hammock with a groan and then informed me, "In all the excitement I forgot to take my quinine. I think my malaria has returned."

I did not understand her ghosts but I watched her carefully. For some time it seemed that for two suns out of every seven she could do little and to cool her body she would sit on a rock with her feet in the shallows of the river while we talked.

"Do you know the story of The First Argument?" she asked me. "It was one of my father's favorites."

I nodded. "My mother told it to me when I was a child."

Arana beamed. "Oh, good! Let me tell you how I heard it."

"In the early days of the earth before the invention of silence everything could speak. Rocks talked, stones spoke, and brooks murmured. Even the sunset spoke. The first thing the sunset said was 'I'm bleeding to death.'

'That's just like the sunset,' a cloud responded. 'Using other people while expecting their sympathy.'

'So high and mighty,' said the bottom of a well.

'She'll cry wolf once too often,' said a vein of gold. 'I'm prettier, but I'm still obscured by a lot of dirt.'

The sunset was about to answer when she was distracted by a bitter dispute.

A beautiful creature neither male nor female, wearing a rainbow of blood and carrying over its shoulder a scythe sharpened by stars, was arguing with earth.

'Who ever heard of life without death?' the beautiful creature demanded.

'I did,' the earth said.

But at last they agreed to put their argument to a vote. They summoned the secants of solstices and the lost motions of lava, and time itself agreed to take the millennia of the meeting.

But nothing happened. Life and death became angry and lapsed into silence. Even now they refuse to discuss the subject and their ears do not receive the audacity of the others' speech.

'It's hard to be a stone,' the rockslides tell them.

'I'm bleeding to death,' the sunset whispers.

'The sky is so small,' says the bottom of a well."

We gazed at each other, content in our mutual connection with the past.

"Do you know the story of the man with the ugly voice who killed and ate the bird with the beautiful song?" I asked her. "He thought if he killed the bird and ate it then he could sing a song like the bird's which could enchant an entire forest."

She smiled. "I know that story," she went on quickly. "He killed the bird and ate it. Then he found his voice was uglier than ever." But she saw that I did not return her smile and she stopped. "I'm sorry. I didn't mean to interrupt you. What happened?"

I paused and gave her a level look that was beyond irritation.

"Well, what happened?"

"Not what you thought. The next day he went out into the forest and sang. His voice was beautiful. His voice was like the bird's."

"That's a strange story. Does it have a cannibal meaning? Does it mean if you eat something you possess it?"

And this time it was I who smiled. "Again you are wrong. He sang with the beauty of the bird. But the ears of men and animals had turned to stone. The leaves of the trees fell off and lay unhearing on the ground. The forest had gone deaf."

She laughed. "That's an ending beyond the ending."

"Speaking of endings," I said, "do you know what I want to be if I die?"

"I didn't think you believed in life after death."

"I don't. I believe in death after death. But much of that that seems alive is dead."

She thought that over. After a while she said, "All right. What do you want to be?"

"A shark."

"You want to be a shark?" she said in a surprised manner.

"I do."

A small cloud passed over us and then the sun shined as brightly as before. Breezes carrying the scent of flowers moved a lock of her hair.

"Yes. And I'll tell you why. You see, what we call the Lake of the World is really an ocean."

She started to interrupt with "I know all that..." but I stopped her.

"An ocean is vast," I continued. "And what do you think dirties that vastness?" I saw her shrug her shoulders. "Lies! No lie disappears. It floats forever. Lies never sink. They don't have the decency of stones. Stones sink through the water and disappear. Stones tell the truth. But lies! They turn everything ugly and they float on the top of the ocean, filthy, distorted, deceiving."

I could see she was about to say something and I quickly continued.

"So I'll tell you why I want to be a shark. I will swim under the water and when I see a lie I will attack it like the great shark of the deep waters. I will rip its legs off. I will cut its torso in two. I will not eat them, but I will swim around them watching them bleed in the water and die. They will bleed a lot. A lie has the blood of more than one human being in it."

Now I felt the breeze in my own hair. The scent of frangipani drifted past and now I saw her looking at me with a special light in her eyes. She laid her hand on my arm.

"Brother..."

"Yes?"

"Brother of Cloud in the Water..."

I waited. I knew by her look that she was going to speak from the spirit inside her and like a ray of sunlight it was possible that her spirit was more direct than mine.

But she couldn't discover the phrase. The fine thing she was going to say ended lamely.

"Oh.... I don't know.... You love truth so much.... I have such an admiration..."

"I like truth better than lies."

She was disappointed. She felt I should have used the word 'love'.

"You love truth," she informed me.

I shook my head. But I regretted it. I could see I had shocked her.

"Truth...," I began. Then I stopped before I said something important.

"What?"

"Nothing," I replied.

11

The mosquitoes were getting worse and someone had put new sandalwood on the fire. The crackling of the logs helped me to continue with my thoughts.

Arana not only knew the magic of our language but she had brought with her a special box that made sounds we had never before heard, and there were two that she knew I liked more than the others.

"What would you like to hear today?" she would ask me with a sparkle in her eyes. "Sibelius' *Valse Triste* or Brahms' *Clarinet Quintet*?"

I would nod at both names and she would laugh. Lifting the top of the mysterious box, she would place a round flat black object inside it which was held down by a jointed piece of wood with an end on it that looked like an odd bird's beak. Then she would make small circular movements with her right arm and the noises would begin.

Many of my tribe did not like the plain new box and felt that our conch shells and especially our carved drums which were painted in black, red and white had the best sounds. The drums had great meaning to their makers, having been carefully selected from special woods which were hollowed out by slowly blowing air over hot coals laid inside them, then fitting the tops with live snake or lizard skin secured by gum and adding special designs with human teeth. Each gave them the noises they wished.

"How can I call my wife back from the garden with that?" they complained of the box.

"It is a woman's toy. No warrior can talk to another warrior with it."

Even though she explained that the sounds were for pleasure and not for communication, most of the tribe did not want to listen to it. But the younger children delighted in directing squealing noises at the box through doubled leaves. The older boys had a contest to see who could play the loudest bamboo flute. They cut big stems, being careful to leave the partition on one end, and then squabbled over which flute sounded better, blowing through one hole near the end or none. Even the Wind From the West joined in one evening with soft sounds coming through the tallest piece of slit bamboo leaning outside a hut.

The sky woman did not seem to tire in watching these games but she seemed pleased when I asked her if she wished to meet my father.

"Of course I would." Then she whispered to me, "I thought he was dead."

"He is in the Middle World," I told her. I did not feel the need to tell her why I had invited her, that I was hoping the sky woman's spirit might aid him on his journey.

She took her round woven hat down off a peg in the hut and when she had it on sometimes the only way I could tell which way she was going was to look at her feet. It had a thick, turned-down brim which was just a little longer in the back than the front and the underside cast a green light onto the pale skin of her face.

As we walked away from the village my heart felt a momentary sadness once more. I remembered that in the evenings we had kept the doors of our huts tightly closed after his passing so that his ghost would not feel it had to remain for our sake and that it would find the right road to Adiri. For one moon I had smeared my body with charcoal and kept a vigil with my father in his hut during the daylight, wrapping him in his favorite mats, and smoking his body over a fire. In her own sadness, my mother had sat under the hut, smearing his dripping fluid over her nude body while her sister attended her in her Unclean Hours. Then he was carried in his cross-legged position and placed in a bamboo chair on the burial mountain.

Davey

Today, when we reached the top of the peak, a distance to the west from our village where the moon and the sun go down, my heart had calmed and I was pleased to see that his body was still sitting as I had placed him in the fourth highest of the five ledges.

"He's bright red," Arana commented, somewhat surprised.

"The women anointed his body with coconut oil and then he was painted with ochre before he was brought up the Skeleton Ladder."

For some reason I could see her comparing his wide cheekbones to mine, which were much narrower. But she studied all the people in my tribe with extra interest and I thought it only natural. His broad nose which still held the claw of a ferocious cassowary seemed, to me, to be still inhaling the perfumed flowers of the lands below us.

"This reminds me of a poem written by a man of beautiful words who lived in my country about four hundred years ago. He wrote:

> 'Sleep after toil,
> Port after stormy seas,
> Ease after war,
> Death after life does greatly please.'"

Protected under a sloping formation, my father was leaning back against the rock wall, propped up with strong arrows and flanked on either side by the bones of his relatives while he looked out over the tops of the trees.

"Do you think his spirit after life is pleasing him?" I asked without trying to make the question sound important.

She was silent for a moment. Raising her head she gazed up through the blue sky at the fluffy clouds above us. Then she looked back at me.

"The spirit of your father who died defending The People of the Only World has followed the ancient route of Sido, the first death ever to occur, and ascended directly to the sky to live with Hiovaki, the Great Spirit of War. With your help he has successfully traveled to the Last World."

I breathed a silent sigh of relief for I knew that the sky woman was telling me the truth. Never had I told her the story of my father's

Brother of Cloud in the Water

passing in the Battle for the Cassowary Feathers. Yet she knew. Furious as I had been with her after the Battle of the Orchid Spider, I was certain that she would have special knowledge about the sky where she lived with its sun, moon and stars and the winds which could suddenly change from mild breezes to winds that could topple a tree in an instant. I was glad that I had brought her to the special mountain.

"Your father has different features than yours," she commented carefully.

"He is actually my second-father, the man who raised me," I told her. "But the shape of his face and that of my first-father are alike in many ways."

"One of your elders mentioned to me that you are a Child of Special Birth."

"I was born twelve months after my first-father died," I said proudly. "He is on the ledge above us. May I have a piece of your hair to leave with him?" I asked.

"Of course," she said. "It would be an honor," and without any hesitation she stood very still as I cut off a wondrous red lock and carefully wrapped it up in a leaf.

"Oranooa told me some exciting news," she continued. "He said that my father was a guest of your mother and first-father and that he stayed to help your mother in her grieving. Isn't it amazing that now we have also met?"

I nodded. This was something I had not known and would have to think over.

She was looking around at the other ledges. "Are these all loved ones?" she asked.

"Every one," I told her.

"What do you do with the others?"

"Very sick people are thrown in the river when they die and their spirits float out to the Lake of the World. And if it happens that two children are born at the same time to the same mother then one is buried here."

"You mean the family keeps only one child alive?"

"Yes. It is a bad omen. Besides, the dead relatives long to care for the soul of the second child."

"How do you know these things?"

"They come to us in our dreams. Some of my tribe will come up here to sleep close to their family so that they may visit them in their dreams and receive knowledge that they had not had before."

"And what about non-loved ones?"

"If someone is killed in a private quarrel, it is the duty of his brother or uncle to kill that man and throw him to the crocodiles. The spirit of a murderer becomes an outcast from all other spirits. They are doomed to live in a swamp in the bush from which they can never escape. Try as they might to struggle to step out, they are only to be dragged down again into the bog, rising and sinking forever."

"I guess I should watch out for swamp ghosts," she said with a smile.

"No," I corrected her. "It is the bad spirits to watch out for. The spirit of a murderer is not a ghost. Ghosts can be spirits of brave men, like my father, who have died in a fight. Murderers are cruel spirits, vicious spirits to be avoided forever. You will know him from the blood which has spurted from his body for it shines like a fire at night. He devours his victims and cannot be killed with an arrow, only frightened away by rattling a handful of poisoned arrows at him."

"Then we had best be returning before sunset," she commented. "Have you ever tried writing the bad spells for others on the bottom of your feet?"

"Why would I want to do a dangerous thing like that?"

"It would not be dangerous for you. It would mean that with each step you would be stamping out their evil and rubbing it into the ground."

"Is this idea yours?" I asked suspiciously.

"No. You should know by now that I'm not a sorcerer. It's an old Middle Eastern habit, from another people far away from here."

Again she was asking me to believe that, unseen on the Lake of the World, more potential enemies lurked, and it made me more worried than ever. But suddenly I heard a wondrous noise not far away and I leaped to my feet.

"Come! The Birds of Paradise are dancing!"

I raced down the mountainside, grabbing onto thick lianas to slow my sliding while I pushed the leafy ferns from my path. The sky woman crashed her way down the slope behind me and when she came to a stop she was dripping with sweat and breathing heavily.

"Did you have to...to run so fast?" She started to rub her seat where she had apparently fallen more than once.

I just shook my head at her womanliness and motioned her to sit quietly on the forest floor.

Out of breath but never without words, she began to say, "Where are... ?"

Quickly I silenced her with a finger to my mouth and pointed upward to the topmost branches of my favorite tree, the one passed down through generations of our family and which was now mine.

A series of seven caws rang out, followed by a single one, as one male called to the females, and these sounds were repeated by a second male bird challenging the first.

Cahr, cahr, cahr, cahr, cahr, CAHR, cahr. CAHR. Cahr, cahr, cahr, cahr, cahr, CAHR, cahr. CAHR.

Along the highest limbs, the males hopped along the clear branches in a courtship dance that even our best warriors liked to copy. We could see their dark bodies and brilliant yellow caps bobbing up and down as we watched them dancing through the leaves. Each time the bird would utter the final CAHR, it would dip its head downward, throw its two golden-marked wings in front of its body and fan its fabulous red tail feathers up and outward as it momentarily froze for effect. Two thin ornamental feathers in white dangled down on either side of his tail feathers and seemed to be equally attractive to the smaller reddish-black females flying in for a look before the mating.

"Oh, my!" the sky woman sighed after watching the birds. "They're absolutely stunning!" She looked at the bird arrows in my right hand. "You're not going to shoot one are you?"

The critical tone of her voice made me change my mind from what had been my first choice of action. I shook my head. "The Bird of Paradise is my totem."

"Really?" she exclaimed. "It is mine also, given to me by my father."

"As it was with me," I informed her. "It is our continuing line between the past and the present, more sacred and binding than blood-kinships."

"And maybe doubly-so," she said.

I did not understand her meaning.

A introspective and almost sad expression passed across her face and then she changed the subject. "Do you know the story about the Phoenix bird?"

I shook my head.

"A long time ago, even before the ancient Greeks, there was a bird that flew in to a land called Phoenicia from the east once every five hundred years. It would build a nest in the palm trees, light the nest on fire and vanish along with its nest. But three days later the same bird would appear reborn, collect the ashes in an egg-shaped leaf and fly to Heliopolis in Egypt where it would place the ashes as a gift to the Temple of the Sun. Then it would sing to the Sun before it flew eastward once more for another five hundred years. This is where the phrase, 'To rise Phoenix-like from its ashes' originated. Isn't that interesting?"

"The bird sounds as if it could have been a Bird of Paradise, but our birds come back every year."

"It's a good story about overcoming adversity, about persevering against odds. You do that all the time. You told me how your tribe started to question your leadership even after you found them the flying thunder bird."

"Will another Bird of Ghosts bring us gifts?" I asked her hopefully.

"I don't know. The war is almost over."

"What war?"

"The Second World War. The First World War was supposed to be the 'War to End All Wars' in this century, but that did not happen."

"We are the People of the Only World. There is only one other tribe on our island (perhaps another if I believe the ancestors, I said to myself) and we are always at war. This is A Forever War, not a first one or a second one, or even a third one."

"Well, in that regard, your country is no different than any other, that's for sure."

"Then why won't more Birds come?"

"They might," she replied. "But I wouldn't plan on it."

"People always quarrel. Enemy tribes always quarrel. No one is ever content," I said countered bitterly. "There will be more battles. There will be more Birds of Ghosts."

"For you and for your tribe's sake, I hope so," she said kindly. "And you're right, as usual."

"About what?"

"People being judgmental. There are even some people in The Outside World who consider your style of life to be 'primitive by virtue of simple technology', but I have never agreed with that."

"What are you talking about?"

"They look down on you because you have no written language."

"A mind is brighter if it has to remember everything," I countered, slightly annoyed by this invisible criticism.

"I have the same opinion. Illiteracy, after all, is only an accident of whereabouts. I would have been illiterate if I had been brought up here. That would not have meant I would have had a mind any less exact than yours, and yours is excellent."

I was pleased with her compliment but did not let her know it. She continued.

"To be termed "primitive" because your life is not filled with technology seems to me to be a poor definition. A better one would be people living in regions where the tremendous exigencies of nature had dominated their lives for so many centuries that the possibility of enjoying enough leisure to create non-mythical reflection which could then turn into non-subjective thought such as engineering inventions like the wheel, speech inventions like writing, and explanations of phenomenon like philosophy rather than myth or religion, had been denied them due to isolation from others as well as the constant necessity of coping with savage environments. You might go so far as to say that their past did not create their present. Rather it is their present which keeps on creating their past."

She had been talking so fast that my mind was racing to comprehend the words she was saying but everything ended up in a blur of new phrases I only partially understood. However, by the tone in her voice, I felt her goodwill. Except for my wife, she was the only woman I had known who possessed a gaiety and interest in the world about her.

Swooping past us a black and green butterfly as large as my hand settled heavily on a bush with spear-shaped leaves and gingerly walked over to feed on clusters of pink flowers which had deep throats and yellow centers.

Finally I replied.

"The arrow of time has no point. It is now."

12

All these thoughts were suddenly interrupted.
"What was so bad about that day?" someone said.
"The second part of the battle was not one to be proud of."
Objections were coming from many voices.
"You mean it is bad to win a battle?"
Despite ourselves we now glanced from the warriors' skulls on their shelves of black palm and mangrove to the softwood shelf on which we kept the skulls of the women.
My friend stopped stroking the pig. He slipped the rope off its foot and with the pig still cradled in his arms he stood up and walked out the door.
I could not believe that the disputes were all beginning again and swiftly I touched my loin cloth where I had hidden the claw of the warrior animal. Then I told myself it was true. I had actually fought a fight to the death with the most tremendous warrior I had ever known and the warrior had turned out to be an animal. I said to myself also that the arrival straight through the clouds of the sky by the Bird of Ghosts severing entire trunks of trees had made an impression upon me not shared by my tribe. They were impressed by smaller magic, by omen birds, by shapes of frenzies on leaves, by the suspicion of sorcery on the part of a companion, not by large things outside of everyday life. Tonight I knew the women would be in mourning for the death of the trees. That was the custom. The women believed they were descended from trees, but no one would think about the typhoon that killed the trees and yet had spared their descendants.

Davey

My hand was still bleeding and as I held it up to look at it I was conscious of the critical looks of a number of younger warriors. I had forgotten that the Battle of the Orchid Spider had not been so long ago. I knew why they were so resentful. Although the second part of the plan had not been mine, they disliked the way it had all been turned upside down with the interference by the Woman With Hair the Color of Blood who, for some reason, they considered to be my responsibility, and even more important than that, they had not gotten over their anger that I had not altered the plan to allow them to take captives. They had wanted some women alive.

The husband of my wife's sister entered the doorway carrying a large clam shell filled with warm water and camellia leaves. He picked up the clay pots and put them outside and then sat down among the other men and everyone watched me sticking the camellia leaves on my skin. The leaves stuck to my skin for awhile and then fell off.

"You need the Healer of the Flesh," Mbugo told me. "The Man of New Bodies."

But I was stubborn and said no, this was not serious enough for him.

"He will burn the tails of fish and the tails of animals and blow the smoke on you. He will make white magic to combat the black magic of sickness."

I shook my head.

"His father failed to cure Oola," I said bitterly. "I am glad that man went out of his mind and was sickened from taking his own medicine. Killing him was a pleasure."

"He may have failed to get the bad spirits out of your wife's lungs, but now his son has taken his place and he knows new magic."

"My illness is not worthy of him."

"It is for you to say!"

"Yes. And anyway..."

"What do you mean, 'anyway'?"

"I mean that anyway he should try his art on my friend Anoogaro."

"What? You *must* be sick! Anoogaro has Twilight of the Flesh."

"He should be killed," an old man said.
Then another added, "We have always killed them. That is the cure. Kill them and throw them to the crocodiles. But you stopped us. You stopped him from being cured."
"Yes. And I will continue to. Anoogaro is wiser than I am." I did not tell them, but even the sky woman had agreed with me. She had not been distressed to see him with his rattan mask covering his face with no nose and she had complimented his wife on the intricate design she had woven upon hers.
"Leprosy may disfigure the body, but not the mind." I knew she was making light of their malady to make them feel better when she said, "If you drew black marks around your red blotches, you would really have a unique pattern!"
For once the men did not continue to argue and after awhile we made preparations for the dance of the women. We posted warriors on the trails far away from the dance and when it was almost dark we sat in silence with bark hoods over our heads and I felt my skin start to ooze again because there was no warmth in the long house and everything felt wet and damp. We were not allowed a fire because the women were in mourning for the death of the ancestral trunks from which their legs had emerged as boughs and their wrists and their ankles had been born as twigs. We knew that the rustling of the leaves was their hair and we were obliged to remain in silence without food.
The women had mysteries of their own and knew medicinal plants we did not and this was the one special time they had ascendancy over us. Not even our ancestors had seen the women dance but despite that rumors had reached us. In the long ago perhaps some child had taken a forbidden look at the Dance for the Trees, some child who became old and was already dead, and the tales had been passed down among the men. We knew the dance took place in the dark and the stories of ancestors told us that the women danced naked after a storm had killed their trees, and then sounds of leaves rustling and twigs cracking were followed by cries. So we sat in the darkness with the black hoods over our heads and after a while we found we were listening acutely to the sound of twigs snapping and

at last the murmur of women's voices and their voices did not sound like the voices we heard every day.

Suddenly a shriek tore through the darkness and in spite of myself I felt the hair stand up on my spine. Then outside the long house we heard the sound of feet shuffling in short and unnatural steps and I thought I detected the swishing of leaves through the air. The strange steps began to intermingle with the regularity of small branches being broken and then another wild and mournful cry pierced the darkness of the long house and faded away. I had only been present at the Dance for the Trees one other time in my life. I had been a boy and I had been tied to the center post of our house and our dogs had also been tied by the feet and muzzled with tight strands of creeper and only the pigs were outside for fear they would eat us. But the pigs were in their pens bolted fast by mangrove branches and I had seen my mother give them a large meal of taro root which would last them through the night. As I thought of that I knew now why we were not hearing the excited barking of dogs or the cries of children.

A wave of silence engulfed the sounds we had heard and we remained rigidly unmoving wondering what was happening. But following the quiet a slight swell of sound occurred and at first it was very low but bit by bit it grew louder though we could not make out the words. The women were chanting and occasionally we thought we heard something we recognized and then it faded away into the swishing and the short, convulsive steps, always followed at intervals by the snapping of twigs. Then a new sound rose from the village and grew louder and louder and it raced toward us like a tidal wave on the sea. With one voice the women were sending a long moan into the night filled with pain and grief for their dead ancestors. But that too died away and close to the long house we heard sounds that were whistling yet which ended subdued as though long twigs still green with life were whipping the women's flesh. No noises of pain occurred, only the swishing of twigs through the air and their absorption by the flesh of the women.

And at that time when we were thinking of the women's flesh the only other rumor any man had heard even from ancestors was that for the women to touch each other was taboo. The same tale had told us that the women were allowed to touch only trees. We did not know that this was true but we believed it because the dance was sacred and it celebrated the source of the women themselves. Many moons ago, so many that they were like pebbles on the shores of the sea, we had heard that in daylight one woman had been found with her thighs parted by a small sapling, as though she had been dragged there by the other women, and her head had been comfortably placed upon the white pith of a palm lying beneath it on the forest floor. That story too was from the days of myth from the times that had been concerned with the crimes of creation, and we had heard that the white pith had drunk her blood because it had changed color and had turned to pink, and in her throat dividing her body from her partly detached head, a knife of wood, propped up by a twig, had been left in her severed windpipe.

We did not dare to ask because this was a mystery which belonged to women only. As I sat there with the hood of darkness over my head and thinking of these things I forgot my bleeding skin and I knew it was somehow indecent to continue to treat my wounds with camellia leaves. Without fire it had become cold in the long house and for a moment I had the strange thought that only when engaged in an ambush or the silence preceding a raid or the stealth of hunting had warriors ever been this still. And I was surprised to find that I did not dislike it. I had trained myself to patience and it takes patience to think. But I moved myself slightly so that my spine was resting against a post. And now that I was more comfortable I told my mind to stay as still as forest swampland so it would not impede a sudden thought which like a reddish rail might wish to find some secret bird's way over lily pads and through thickets.

The inside of the long house was black and under my bark hood it was even blacker and I knew that outside the dark night was only lighted by the stars. I felt that the blackness was right and the women had chosen the right time and then I remembered my dream the night of the typhoon. For an instant only I saw that great white breast of the moon shining with a silver light I had not seen before and it occurred to me that men were from the day and women from

Davey

the night and that women had existed long before men. My thought told me that men were associated with fire and fire penetrated the darkness with its light. Ancestors after ancestors had passed to us the legend of our birth as men and when I had been younger I had gone looking for it on our highest mountain. No one living had seen it. Men were twins, the legend told us, and once long ago beyond our minds to imagine all men had been born from fire. The tale of the ancestors told us that our biggest mountain, which was so old that it had white hair, had opened one night and though it looked like a woman giving birth it was not. Man did not have an ancestor mother. He was born with a loud cry and a great tear swept across the sea crying for the sorrow of the birth of man and where the huge tear of man swept there death followed. And even before he was being born he had killed many women because as the great tear for the birth of man crested above the trees sweeping in from The Lake of the World most of the trees from which the women descended were wrenched from the earth and destroyed.

Now I was more still than before and I knew then that the legend had not lost its power to horrify me. And slowly as a bat on a branch opens its wings to feel with its flesh the support of the air my memory expanded and this myth from the past bore my thoughts back to the horror of my origin. For I had sprung from fire and my name was not Brother of Cloud in the Water. My name was man. And here in this double darkness with the women outside mourning for the Death of the Trees I told myself how much more hideous was my birth. For with a groan that shook the night a wound of fire had opened wide on the mountain and then spurts of flame had seared everything around them and at last in his flesh of orange a stone man had emerged as flowing fire and descending from the loftiness of the mountain he had run down its flanks in molten rivers that destroyed everything they touched.

Then his twin the sun had been hurled beyond him above the darkness of the night. But the rivers of stone blackened and man's heart became cold and was not like the heart of his brother still burning in the sky. And oppressed by this myth I felt my lips moving with the speech of silence and I told myself that now I knew why death turned man to dust. He had been born from stone.

13

Borne by gentle breezes rising around us the chants of the women blended into a wordless murmur which interrupted my imaginings and I felt myself waiting for my memory of this myth to die. Then the whispers again turned into cries and at last into shrieks but the terror of my birth still absorbed me. For I had been born without a mother. And the wound on the mountain from which I had dripped like blood had belonged to no woman and I had come from nothing and nowhere in my history as a man was some ancestor I might touch who was less hard than stone.

The thought depressed me and I decided I would not let this secret swamp bird steal any further into the thickets of myth and I tried only to listen to the women. I was almost grateful for these sounds of intensity but as I listened to them I noticed suggestions of frenzy that I had not heard before. Their shrieks became rhythmic and then I wondered if I detected a note of ecstasy because the sound of branches beating and twigs whipping flesh was louder and more violent and the air itself seemed to throb with shrieks and the cries of women mingling with the fast rustling of leaves.

The arrival of daylight was like a deliverance and we took the hoods off our heads and went outside. The women had disappeared and the village seemed deserted. Not a child had been released and we saw no dogs sniffing for food or wandering aimlessly around the houses. We were still cold from the night and as the sun rose higher we moved into the rays and avoided the shadows. The sound of our breathing was labored because the rattan hoods long unused had been musty and the damp air that all night long our lungs had struggled to draw through the hoods had brought us heavy odors of cold ashes and smoked skulls and the blackened mandibles of pigs. There had been no odor from the new rushes on the roof and they did not possess the reek that came from sacred masks and bones and the tanned skin of enemies which we kept for magical purposes. And in our nostrils stale fumes of tobacco smoked by men of flesh or long ago by men of bone lingered now and increased the difficulty of breathing.

Suddenly the fresh air acted on me in a way I had not expected and I broke out in a fit of sneezing. I had expected this before and I had been surprised it had not occurred when the hood had been over my head during the dance of the women. I had been too long without breathing deeply and I told myself that my sneezing was caused by the contrast of fresh air with tobacco fumes that had entered even the grain of wood in our long house. I was the only man who did not smoke and the warriors no longer thought it impolite not to offer me tobacco.

The sneezing passed and my nose cleared and then odors of orchids fallen along with the trees on which they had grown began faintly to reach me and at last their scents were disturbed by the sudden smell of a pig pen. Then the sharpness of crushed eucalyptus leaves overwhelmed the smell of the pigs and for a moment I wondered if the women had used eucalyptus in their Dance for the Trees.

I sat in the dust and looked up at the shark still hanging from a tree but like the other men I was only waiting for the women to emerge from their houses. Over the wreckage caused by the storm and through the forest still standing beside it the loud call of a bird sounded with surprising harshness.

The first to come forth from the houses were the dogs and for a while they searched the ashes of the cooking fires for vegetable skins and then they went and settled themselves in the sunshine. Boys followed, but they avoided us and started rolling a coconut covered with fruit gum. They began shouting and trying to hit it by hurling little bamboo spears. We sat in the warmth of the early rays watching the dogs scratching fleas and making friendly bets as to which animal would be the next to pick up its hind foot. Then the women walked from the houses and empty string bags were looped round their foreheads with small bags hanging down on top of them and most of the smaller bags contained babies. They were trailed by silent girl children holding onto their grass skirts and some of the women balanced other children on their hips.

Mbugo sat down next to me and stared at the shark. My wife's sister walked toward him and stood there holding their small boy.

"I am going to the garden," she told us.

"This morning I shall cut up the shark," he told me.

They seemed to be on different thought preferences.

"We need food. I think we have sweet potato."

"Brother of Cloud in the Water," he continued. "Remember! My half has the liver."

I nodded and turned toward his wife.

"Are you better?" Aala asked me.

"No. I can't close my hand."

"It's your bow hand too."

"Yes. That is what worries me."

"Then the camellia leaves did no good?"

"They helped. And some help is better than none."

The concerned expression which had come over her face was giving way to an almost imperceptible smile. In order to gain her attention the child at her hip was tugging at the waistband of her skirt. I knew he was shy because he could not speak and I did not wish to confront him even with a glance. I stared over his shoulder and did not try to talk to him but I sensed he was sending a significant look over my shoulder also.

Suddenly the little child broke into song.

"You've been singing to him!" I said to his mother.

"Don't get sweet potato," Mbugo interrupted. "It's stringy. "Get taro root."

I watched her walk off into the light that was casting deep shadows from the trunks and the boughs of the trees. Then I gave the upper half of the shark to the men although I retained the ownership of the teeth and the men kicked the dogs out of the way so that they could start cutting the shark in two. The husband of

Brother of Cloud in the Water

my wife's sister broke his knife on the skin and the men had to wait while he went for another. They knew he had received his half before they had because he had seen fit to tell them so three times and they waited for him with the patience of custom in which I saw traces of irritation.

Suddenly in the blue sky above me I saw a flock of birds flying close together with their black wings beating on both sides of white breasts while behind them long legs the color of faded lotus seeds seemed to float in the air as though they were almost not part of their bodies. They flew in the direction of the garden toward which I had seen Aala walking and as the birds disappeared I sensed that the sight of her had again made me think of a lotus.

I continued to gaze at the sky which seemed now despite its unthreatening blue to be empty and lonely. No noises from a new Bird of Ghosts or the sky woman returning could be discerned. And when at last I lowered my head I saw the trees spared by the storm and they reminded me that Mbugo might think I had made a bad bargain. To exchange half a shark for some taro root and a coconut was not in itself something foolish but then for me to have offered to kill him a tree kangaroo could make such a man imagine that he was capable of outwitting me. And I knew he was stupid enough to think that he was the one for whom I intended its flesh.

"Brother of Cloud in the Water!"

The call had come from the men kneeling around the shark. As I walked toward them, slowly, they stood up with their knives in their hands and the circle parted.

"Look at this! Look at this, Brother of Cloud in the Water."

They had opened the belly of the shark and torn out the intestines and slit its stomach. On the mud drying in the morning sunshine slanting down through the trees gray membranes had exposed something tiny that looked almost human. It had slid forth and now lay like white twigs at our feet.

111

14

I bent down and with my spear hand I reached into the stomach of the shark and emptied its entire contents onto the damp mud. As small as the legs of sparrows a little jumble of bleached bones came out to join the rest but I kept on searching for something else and at last I touched an object no larger than my kneecap. I left it inside until I had arranged the bones in what I thought should be their proper order and then I pulled the last piece of the puzzle from the shark's intestines and placed it at the top of the other bones. The tiny skull above little ribs no larger than a fledgling's told me that despite its lack of size we were looking at something human.

"It's a baby," I said.

"A baby?"

"Yes, the bones of a baby," I declared.

"No baby is that small. We know about babies. Babies are larger than you think."

"It's the ghost of a baby! That is what it is."

I turned to the husband of my wife's sister.

"Do you still want your half of the shark, the half with the liver?"

"No," he said, shaking his head and almost backing away. "This is not good magic. This is bad. And what about you? Do you still want the teeth that killed this baby?"

"If it really is a baby," someone questioned.

"Brother of Cloud in the Water…"

"Yes?"

"That baby is a ghost! It is the baby of a baby."

I was beginning to get spots before my eyes from kneeling down. My bow hand throbbed and sweat ran down my forehead and into my eyes and it stung like the salt water in the Lake of the World. I stood up and tried not to stagger because a wave of dizziness had engulfed me and I was conscious that if I let it sweep me away I would lose the trail of an important thought.

Something told me that this trail might lead to an important victory. And suddenly the little skeleton reminded me of the fact that once I had been an infant myself and that the day I had been born my mother told me a brilliant rainbow had risen right over the clouds and made an arc of wonder over our village. She had said to me that I had been born for great things and she had always been right. Now I knew she was right once again because something told me that I alone knew where the baby came from and as I thought about that I could almost hear the roar of underground rivers in my ears. The rainbow under which I had been born had lifted the green of the jungle to the sky and taken the red color of hibiscus from the earth and the yellow of the butterfly wings from the air and sent me another suggestion as important as the spider inside the orchid.

I staggered but someone braced me and I went on with my thoughts. I had to make an effort not to die. If I died, no one would have these ideas that came to me like rainbows from clouds. But my skin felt as though it was burning and the spots in front of my eyes thickened and darkened. Then I forced consciousness to return to myself and suddenly my mind felt clear.

The men were scooping the intestines together and stuffing them back into the shark and as I watched them they started to pick up the tiny bones of the skeleton and put them back inside the shark as well. I stopped them.

"Wait! I am responsible for this," I said. "I know what to do. Cut off the jaws of the shark. Build a bamboo platform above the reach of the dogs and people. Put the jaws of the shark on the platform and build another beside it. Place the bones of the baby on the second platform by itself."

"If it is a baby," the same man grumbled again.

"Listen! You will have to do this for me. There is no skin left on my bow hand. I killed the shark and its insides are mine to distribute."

"Then you are responsible for a ghost. The baby of a baby is a ghost."

"You are repeating yourself. I heard you the first time. There are many kinds of ghosts. You should know that. This baby is not bad. You should be concerned about the shark, if anything."

"Then why keep the jaws?"

"Because we keep skulls. The jaws of a shark are its skull."

I waited till they built the platforms and I stayed until they had placed everything as I had asked. I was glad it was a beautiful day and I lingered awhile watching the strong sunlight drying the jaws of the shark and the bones of the baby. For some reason the strength of the sunlight pleased me and I knew if I could recover from what was the matter with me that I could take the delicate tips of strangler vines and tie the tiny skeleton together and then fasten it to a frame of bamboo and that way it would be unbreakable.

I told the men to throw the rest of the shark in the river and when they were through I took an arrow of mine from the long house and between the two platforms I forced it into the moist earth with its point upward. On this magic arrow never intended to be fitted to a bowstring I had previously cut thirty-two notches and now the women and children as well as the men and the warriors would know that I had declared both platforms taboo.

At last I was satisfied and once again I made my way to the long house and started to lie down on my mat. But as I did so I heard something crash to the floor and I was surprised to find that the sound had been caused by my own body falling. Luckily I had fallen onto the mat and as I lay there alone in the darkness I tried to force myself to sleep. But sleep does not come that way for sleep too is a ghost and its dreams are ghosts of a ghost.

Then a certain silliness came over me. I told myself that I ought to go outside and tell that fool who said that the baby of a baby is a ghost that if he wanted to feel the ghost of a ghost he should go to sleep. I tried to push myself off the mat with my bow hand but the hand gave way and I lifted it up in the dim light to look at it as I had done once before. Nothing could be seen but white ulcers and

Brother of Cloud in the Water

it seemed to me strange because my hand is not white. I lay there expecting sleep to come for I could not believe that any man this tired would be unable to sleep. But my mind was keeping me awake and when I told it to stop thinking it paid no attention to me but went on with its thoughts as though I did not exist.

For it was enchanted with its own imagination and it would not allow me no rest. It told me that my body was nothing and the thing in me which counted was my mind. So I lay without rest while my mind still excited by its powers of association went on telling me that seeing the belly of a shark hiding the bones of a baby was part of a chance meeting of that one storm picking just that one shark up from the river and dropping it into one murky pool that only I would happen to cross unexpectedly. And my mind was not content to surrender its triumph to dreams. For once had it not heard when still very young the stray remark of an ancestor who had said something that no one admitted? And I knew that this mind, which today was so proud to stand apart from my body as though it did not wish to associate with a thing that might die, was about to bring words back from the past and was going to whisper in my ear to prevent me from sleeping. Then it told me that the shark had given me the bones of a baby that I intended to return.

I was startled by that word and I wondered to whom I would return the little skeleton until my mind circled and forced me to remember the remark of the ancestor. Now his voice was only an echo which is the ghost of a sound but what made the echo interesting was that he had denied something. Children remember denials and I had been a child. He had denied that there were more than two tribes living in the Only World and he had become angry when someone had said there were three. He became as angry as people do when confronted by truth. He had denied that there was a third tribe living in the Only World, a people whose heads came only to our waists, a people who lived under ground.

Suddenly I sat up with excitement. For once in the part of our country sunken beneath the plains I thought I had had a glimpse of tiny people living under the ground among stones which though broad at the base were sharp at the top like knives. Above them their

115

enemies could die of thirst on the dry savannas because the water drained from the earth into underground rivers I had thought I had heard roaring beneath me.

Silently I began having a conversation with myself. I was convinced that our enemies across the mountain now had a new war chief since we ambushed them and he was the best they had ever had. Suppose I could make friends with these people who lived underground and suppose they could help me capture this fight leader and carry him away. We could learn his new tribal secrets.

My body ached and my skin was forming sores but my mind was now elsewhere. It rejoiced. Now I had a plan that was different from the last. I was glad I had planted my arrow between the platforms and thus declared them taboo, and I gazed at the door and outside the sun was now shining after a shower that had cleansed the bones and I knew the heat was also drying the slime of the shark from the baby.

"Good!" I said to myself.

I lay back on the mat and felt a wave of pain pass over me but before the next one arrived I told myself that if I lived through my sickness this magic was good. For I knew who that baby was. He was a tiny infant who had had only a moment of life and there was a reason he was so small. His mother was a pygmy.

15

In the early dawn of the next morning, just before the White Eye of Night usually closed, before the first twittering of the birds began, and before any other person had thought to rise, I quietly gathered my lightest bow and smallest arrows in my left hand and nervously crept out of the long house. I felt too weak to carry anything heavier than the baby's bones and I hoped no warrior would try to join me or perhaps even attempt to stop me from going. Every movement I made seemed too loud and I was sure someone would notice. Such a feeling I had never had before. In the past when I had left quietly to hunt or to patrol our lands I had been healthy and relatively certain of my return. But this time, even though I was certain of my cause, I did not know if I had the strength to accomplish my ideas and I was working against even my own instincts for survival.

I could hardly stretch my muscles which had stiffened rather than relaxed during my rest but my mind seemed a little stronger than the night before and I didn't feel as dizzy as I had previously. Painfully I walked in the direction of the caves and caverns, toward a people that the ancient elder denied, wondering how to find them.

The dampness of the forest floor felt refreshing on the soles of my feet but I could tell with every step where each wound was located. I must have looked like a person crippled with age as I used first known paths, and then moved onto unknown ones. A light persistent rain was my only companion for over three days. White mists were covering the foothills, and as I climbed higher I could see that low clouds were also sleeping on the highest ridges. I headed toward a series of blue mountain ranges that I had once pointed out to the sky woman, one of which she had said was in the shape of a saddle. She had kneeled down and drawn me a picture in the dirt of the animal she called a horse and explained the use of the saddle and why the shape of the mountain was called a saddleback.

I must admit it. Except for Oola, my wife, women have been something to stay away from; women are dangerous! But now I miss Arana's stories. She told me amazing tales that I still do not believe. One story was about the light from the sun and that it supposedly takes millions of moons to travel here to where I wait for it each morning, depend upon its warmth, figure on its angles when I wish to surprise an enemy, and enjoy feeling its power. She said that I was experiencing the past while living in the present.

When I told her that as a child I had seen a Bird of Paradise in the night sky with a long crimson tail she told me that I would see the same bird again if I lived long enough, that it moved like many animals I knew and kept flying round and round above me on the same path over and over again on its own game trail. This has not yet come true.

On the fourth afternoon I had to stop earlier than I had wished for once again I was feeling faint. As I leaned my back against a tree I remembered another story that the Woman with Hair the Color of Blood had told me. In one of those faraway countries she maintained existed, a mother had innocently picked some lotus tree flowers for her child, not realizing that the tree was really a spirit until she saw blood dripping from the stems. She tried to move but couldn't as bark began to grow upward until it covered her body completely and finally she could only whisper her regrets with the rustling of leaves. I reached back slowly and ran my hand over this tree to see if the trunk was warm to my touch but if it had a woman's spirit inside I had a feeling it was gone, like the sky woman.

Why had she left without a word? Had she too been taken by the tree spirits? Should I search the forests for signs of her? I shook my head. If any spirit had taken her, it would have been a sky spirit. I eased down to rest my legs and I wanted to slowly drift off into sleep but I thought of what Anoogaro, the wise one, had told me.

They had had a long talk just before her departure. He said that she admired me; that she was in love in with me. So why had she not stayed? Only now in my isolated mind did I remember what he had said next. It was such a fantastic theory that I had blocked it from my mind. He had told me that she thought we might have the same father! How could that be true? How could I be the brother of the woman I had been one with? Once again I found it too depressing an idea, but before I put it aside I decided that any relation that I did have with the sky woman would make me not weaker but stronger so I did not dwell on it. Suddenly my mind felt overcome by a heavy fuzziness and I shivered under my cloak until I fell into an exhausted dream world.

I dreamt I was sitting on a mountaintop with the sky woman and we were gazing up at the night heavens and talking about beginnings.

She was saying to me, "You would have liked the Norsemen. Their fierceness ruled the fate of their woman. They believed:

> "Of old there was nothing,
> Nor sand, nor sea, nor cool waves,
> No earth, no heaven above.
> Only the yawning chasm.
> The sun knew not her dwelling,
> Nor the moon his realm.
> The stars had not their places."

Above us a cloudy river of stars flowed northward and she pointed out ones familiar to me but with names that were different than ours. Odd names like Sirius, Procyon, Canopus, Acrux, and Betelgeuse to the East; Rigel, Aldebaran, Alchernar, Fomalhaut, and the Pleiades to the West. I dreamt she told me about a place with a cold kingdom of death to the north and a fiery land to the south where twelve rivers produced steamy clouds of mist. There were so many of these drops of water that the world's first giant came into being and when he was killed earth was made from him and his blood was saved to make the Lake of the World. Sparks from the flaming south were thrown into the heavens for everyone to see. All of mankind's parents were supposedly created from one wondrous male tree of ash which supported the universe with the help of a female tree of elm. In this world there were also dwarfs, secretive craftsmen who lived under the earth and…

From a lying position I sat up suddenly. I thought a human hand had touched me.

Looking around, I saw no one. Then, feeling somewhat exposed, I slid to the backside of the tree, settled among its massive roots and covered myself with large leaves that had fallen to the forest floor. I watched a spider with a white cross on its back weave zig-zag patterns in its web above me while a stick insect with spiny legs and camouflage like a chameleon carefully made its way across my legs before I fell asleep again.

I dreamt that I was looking everywhere for the Lost Tribe. I was thirsty and when I found a river that disappeared straight into the foggy mountainside and saw bats flying in and out of the entrance I decided to follow along the edge of the rushing river as it flowed deeply underground. Before the shadows became too dark I found myself engulfed by The Sky of Stone: great caves of honeycombed limestone which had rocks dripping down from above as well as growing up from the earth.

Suddenly two short warriors stepped out in front of me and blocked my path. They folded their arms across their decorated chests and stood firm. Betel-nut juice had stained their small square teeth a brownish color and sideways across each shoulder they wore woven strings that glowed golden even in the darkness. Each man held a stone-headed club but I could see that the pig tusks they wore in their noses were hanging down over their mouths and I gave an inward sigh of relief for I knew I was outnumbered. This meant that they were at peace for the moment. If the curving tusks had been pushed upward, I would have known that I was in for a fight. Slowly I turned my arrows backward to show that I, too, meant them no harm.

I told the pygmy leader, Tall Grass, about the Battle of the Orchid Spider and the Heads of Whores and that I was convinced that if we could capture the enemy war chief it would be better than killing a hundred of his warriors. I described in our last fight I had seen the beginnings of attempts to shoot arrows at us in flocks like birds flying in the morning. My instinct had warned me that this man had other surprises and I explained to Tall Grass that for both our tribes it was vital to know what they were, that together we could defeat them.

"The enemy would be stunned by such an unexpected attack," he agreed.

"They would think it was magic," I said.

"Why is that?"

I stared downward into his eyes. "You know the extent of your caves and caverns and you could, without doubt," I praised him, "rise straight from the earth like adders do from the sand."

He was pleased with the compliment. "What you say is true."

"We can turn that magic against them and make them think it is black. After we learned his secrets we could return his body to his people with his face fitted once again to his skull but with his skin smoked and reduced to the size of yours and stuffed with nettles and poisonous plants."

"I have wondered for a long time now whether the numbers of our enemies to the north had begun to exhaust the space for their gardens," the pygmy leader commented.

"Of course they have. Even on our side of the island three mountain ranges have failed to make their smoke look as far away as before and despite the distance, it seems more frequent."

"That means they're abandoning their old gardens and burning spaces for new ones."

Suddenly I understood why our own forests had seemed to be filling with more cassowaries and tree kangaroos. They lived on fruit and their forests must be shrinking for some reason. And though we hunted them, we even had more pigs than before, but our hunters had accepted this good fortune without bothering to wonder. Even before this day I had asked myself why, but only suspecting the cause.

The answer was now obvious. The game was being pushed over the mountainside by the pressure of enemy hunting and finally the game had fled its own forests and was starting to enter ours. Soon they would be followed by hunters and then the hunters would be followed by cannibal warriors.

"Only a fool could not foretell this future," I declared. "One day each of our tribes could be surprised by the mass attack of hundreds of enemies."

"How do I know your tribe won't do the same to us now that you know where we are?" he asked me directly.

I handed him the bones of the baby which were carefully covered in banana leaves and tied with lianas. "Does an enemy return good spirits to you?" I asked.

He unwrapped the skeleton in front of everyone. There were little cries from the women and their tiny dogs sneezed instead of barking. Finally they smiled at me in an indirect fashion of acceptance and Tall Grass changed the subject.

"Do you mind taking off your loincloth?"

"It is immodest," I said since behind him I saw many little women crowding forward.

"But the women want it," he insisted.

"Women want a lot of things," I told him.

"With us we do what the women want," he announced in a voice that avoided anger though not irritation and which he saw fit that the women heard clearly.

"So they will not get what they want. One time won't hurt them."

"It will hurt your effort to reach the enemy leader from underground. No pygmy will go with you." He waited a while and then he added, "You have not answered."

"I am thinking," I told him. "With us men have died for immodesty."

"You won't die here," Tall Grass said.

"I must say something to my brother," I informed him.

"I see no brother with you," he remarked.

"He is shining," I replied. "When there is no fog or rain he is always shining." Then I addressed the sun. "You are naked, too. The clouds are not your clothes. So your brother now joins you."

I took off my loincloth. Suddenly I was surrounded by tiny people.

"No!" I said to one of the women.

She drew back but other women came forward. One old woman was shouldering her way through the others with her hand outstretched while a younger woman guided her head.

"What's the matter with her?" I asked Tall Grass.

"She's almost blind," he told me.

"Then keep her away."

"Put on your loincloth," he commanded.

I did so, but the pygmies were silent. "Well, what about it?" I asked. The faces of the pygmy women had gone back to a neutral state. "Are you going with me or aren't you?" I demanded.

"I will let you know," he replied with a haughtiness that did not please me.

"Don't bother!" I said in a more superior fashion. "I will go alone in the morning."

Long after the sun had risen there were still shadows among the limestone spires. But I remained angry and finally I seized my spears and bow and arrows and started to look for Tall Grass. Then from behind the spires I became surrounded by armed pygmies. They were carrying short blowguns and small hatchets of black obsidian.

"So the women decided to let you go," I chided them.

"Oh, no," he told me. "We decided ourselves. We just like to give them pleasure. You pleased them by returning the child and agreeing to their other wish of curiosity. Yesterday you pleased them twice."

16

My eyelids were closed but I felt my lips moving.
"I knew those little bones would be good magic!" I said aloud.
"Of course," a voice replied. "Your instincts are always correct."
I opened my eyes. I shook my head in confusion. Had all this been a dream? The dream world is no different than the non-dream one and what one dreams is the same as truth but now Oranooa and not Tall Grass was standing above me. His appearance after what I had been thinking was strange but not magical.
"How did I get here?" I asked as I wondered if I were really in my own body.
"Your mother bore you, surely you know that."
"No, not that. Instead of being in The Sky of Stone I am back in our long house. How did that happen?"
"The Lost Tribe brought you back to us. You had collapsed from your wounds."
"Then it wasn't a dream to capture Hundred Leaves?"
"No. We were told you captured the enemy fight leader and learned his secrets."
"Did Long Grass tell you that the enemy tribe was practicing to shoot their arrows in a different way?
"New way? There are no new ways, Manosoma. Everything has been tried by the ancestors."
"Maybe. But maybe we have forgotten some of the ways. "Oranooa..." I whispered.
"I'm over here," he said. We had been speaking in the darkness. I heard him reach for the palm petiole to light and I saw him struggle

and slip as he rolled the heavy stone holder toward my mat. The burning palm husks sent light flickering over the thatch of the walls.

"That's what age will do for you!" he remarked.

"Does age bring something along with it?" I asked him.

"Something else, you mean? The old will tell you so."

"I didn't ask the old. I asked you."

"Brother of Cloud in the Water," he said, "that's something I like about you. You won't accept smoke from speech. You want to see fire."

He squatted beside me and for a while we both listened to the fire crackling and the hissing and falling of scorched husks from the torch. My loincloth had loosened because of the swellings in my thighs and though the light hurt my eyes I now turned toward Oranooa and as I did so the claw of the warrior animal that I always carried with me worked loose from the moss in which I had placed it and I felt it slide down my leg and fall on the mat in front of us.

I saw his eyes widen with astonishment. Putting my hand over it I struggled to my feet and slowly walked to my room in the long house. I hid the huge claw the color of tortoise shell in a hollow log under sooty claws still attached to the feet of some charcoal owls I had killed. Then I covered the claws with tail feathers from the purple Bird of Paradise and went back to my mat. I fell when I tried to sit down but at last I straightened out and looked at him once more.

"That's not a crocodile claw," he declared. "Nor one from a tree kangaroo."

I shook my head.

"Then it came from an animal I have never seen. Did you find it or did it come from a fight?"

"A fight," I told him.

"Now I understand your wounds," he said. "It was not only the shark."

He lowered himself from his squatting position and sat down beside me. As he put his arms around his knees and I saw his shrewd and glittering eyes staring at me with a capacity for appraisal that had not dimmed with the years. He leaned forward and in the light burning above him I saw wounds on his shoulders, and though I knew he had battle wounds this was the first time I had ever observed that particular series of scars on his shoulders. They looked as though they had been made by mouths and they were so old they had turned gray with time.

"Brother of Cloud in the Water," he said. "You must not die. If you die, our tribe dies with you. You need the healing power of magic. I am going to send you someone that knows that stones are dust and that the arms of trees grow downward into the darkness of earth. You must breathe the mist of mountain lichens. You must eat magic mushrooms. Your body is failing. It needs the Younger Man of New Bodies. You killed his father and he is afraid of you but let me send for him."

I nodded at last. "I will never forgive his father for letting Oola die as she did."

The instant I thought of Oola other things vanished, the trees of the rain forest, the sunlight on the sea, and once again I had the sensation of being two places at once and not only was I here but I was really sitting beside her in the village.

"How do you feel today?" I had asked her.

"Better...," she attempted to answer.

But something inside her was defeating her attempt and changing her voice, once as clear as the song of the Bird of the Morning Star, into a dull whisper.

"You look better," I told her.

"Yes...," she reassured me.

Her voice terrified me. I could not bear that hollow sound of dull extinction. For her voice no longer vibrated. Instead, the muffled sound that came from her chest seemed echoless, like something beaten on a drum that was filled with flesh.

"Much better," I repeated.

Her suffering showed in her face and like a snail shrinking from danger her flesh had withdrawn from her cheekbones and left them behind. Suddenly I stood up and looked down at her wasted body and I became aware of the bones of her pelvis almost sticking through her skin. I had made a mistake. More than two moons ago I had told myself I would look only into her eyes. For her face began to turn into a skull and her lovely lips tightened into two thin lines while the moon had started to shine in her eyes.

She did not know that the sight of her courage which was too big for her body had stricken me like salt water poured on a plant. I had felt the roots of my being wither and I knew I was not strong enough to remain. I needed to regain my composure and consult once more with the Man of New Bodies. He would visit Oola no longer and she had lain unaided for almost three moons. It made no difference to me that he was angry because his magic had failed and I decided as I stood there that he would visit Oola or he would become a ghost.

I walked toward the house of the Man of New Bodies and I called to him before I went inside. No one answered. I entered anyway and found him sitting on the ground with his son. Snake skins hung from the rafters and the house was filled with a large collection of magic plants and poisons.

Both men had the same stupefied expression. Black saliva ran from their mouths and trickled down their chins. I stared at the father with silent bitterness as I told myself that this was the man to whom I had come in hope of curing Oola.

He picked up a leaf lying beside him and passed it to me. On the green leaf lay a small pile of tan powder.

"Have some snuff. It will make you see clearly."

"No! I don't want any."

He stared at me vacantly.

"Have some snuff," he repeated.

I shook my head.

"Too bad," he muttered and took a pinch. Then he passed it to his son and they both began sneezing.

"I came to ask you a question."

He bent his vacant gaze upon me and made an effort to recapture his dignity. "Ask me your question," he said.

But suddenly I was afraid to ask and I remained silent.

"Are you going to ask or aren't you?"

"Yes." I paused and with desperation in my voice I said, "What is the matter with Oola?"

"She has Child of the Lung."

"What?"

"Child of the Lung. Even men can have it."

"What is it"?

He seemed sobered. Now with his scant gray beard streaked with dark saliva and his thin arms and scrawny neck and the skin which hung loosely upon his body he looked suddenly very old.

"In the time when the stars fell we were cannibals," the old man said. "Often we ate the seeds of the red mangrove. People looked like skeletons then."

"I have heard of it."

"So we ate human bodies. We ate them the same as our enemies do now."

A silence followed. Far away we heard hunting dogs baying in the forest.

"Why are you telling me this?"

"Because sometimes when we opened the bodies we found large masses of flesh growing inside the lungs like children. We found some who had livers as large as the hindquarters of pigs. They too had children. So we threw that flesh away. But my father studied it. He made tea from the bark of the truth plant and drank it. He sharpened his vision with mushrooms and he discovered the secret."

He stopped abruptly as though he were on the brink of telling me something that had to do with black magic. I remained silent. I had asked him a question too loathsome to answer. Like a prophesy the pain of unavoidable death swept through me. And while I waited for him to start speaking, I kept saying to myself, "Oola is going to die." And then something else repeated, "I don't believe it! I don't believe it!"

Suddenly he resumed speaking in a strange and resounding voice.

"So my father discovered this secret. Not all children are in the belly of women. The good kind of child is there, but there is a bad kind and that is a child of evil. A child of evil is caused by the semen

Brother of Cloud in the Water

of ghosts."

I stared at him, horrified. A faint crashing sound came to us from far away. A cassowary was running through the underbrush.

"There must be something you can do," I said finally.

"Nothing," he responded.

"There must be something. Anything!"

"Brother of Cloud in the Water, a child in the lung is death."

"I will not accept that," I said.

"You have to. You have to accept it."

"No!"

"You have to. A ghost has entered the lungs of your wife. He has left evil there and his evil is growing."

Then I felt myself turn into a warrior. I was tired of being a victim.

"Listen to me! Stop taking that snuff. Wait a while, but come before twilight. Give her a treatment."

"What kind of treatment?"

"Any kind of treatment! If you don't come to my house, I will come back to yours. Do you know what I'm saying? Is it getting through the snuff?"

He looked at me and nodded.

"And one more thing," I told him. Bring the barks and roots that help breathing. Magic is everywhere but I want no magic tonight. I want things that help breathing."

"All right," he agreed.

It wasn't until I walked outside that I realized there had been a strange odor inside his dwelling. Men making arrows were sitting outside other houses in the village and they lifted the bamboo occasionally and looked along it to see if the arrows were straight. On heavy logs women were beating bark cloth with stone beaters and sometimes they stopped and ran a sharp splinter of bamboo along the notches carved by flints in the surface of the stone and when they had rid the notches of pulp they began beating again.

As I walked toward my house for some reason the people stopped, looked at me, and then continued with what they had been doing. It was the time in the late afternoon when the evening meal was being prepared while there was still enough light to enjoy eating. Women were visiting back and forth and borrowing embers from other fires. A blue haze of smoke began to hover over the village and in the light which was darkening because the sun had sunk behind the trees I heard the crackling of wood and saw the cooking fires gleaming orange in the bluish shadows.

One woman who was late from the garden came in carrying a light load of sweet potatoes. She was a friend of Oola's and they had played together as children. She was as ugly as Oola was beautiful and her awkwardness was embarrassing to see. Her string bag of vegetables kept slipping from her forehead and when it finally fell on the ground due to her clumsiness she stopped and gave me a stupid smile as though the bag had a life of its own before she swung it back on again. She spoke to me as she went by, something she was not supposed to do, but I knew she was not trying to be seductive. She was just stupid. I remained silent but I stared at her in suppressed though sudden anger. I looked at the slack lips which gave her face a slovenly appearance along with her narrow eyes and I did not hate her then but the fact that she was living while Oola was dying made me hate the world itself. I stood still for a moment and I watched Oola's friend go lumbering off toward her house. As she entered her own doorway once again her bag slipped, this time crashing into a palm frond wall, and she turned around to see if anyone were looking. Then she picked it up and disappeared into her dwelling.

Above the rain forest light clouds the color of pearl shell had been forming and I continued standing there and then I knew that I did not want to see Oola. Not yet anyway. The eight moons of sickness that had gone by had removed something inside me. I asked myself if it was my courage. I was the War Chief of the People of the Only World but now I could not summon up enough courage to return and see Oola die. I raised my head to the sky and I longed for dissolution. I wanted to be part of those clouds or to drift toward the forest like smoke coming from the cooking fires. I thought how painless it would be to become a raindrop and fall into the immensity of the Lake of the World.

Suddenly I strode to the edge of the village and went a little way into the woods and sat down in a clearing. I knew I was trying to get up the courage to go back but I also wanted to continue my thoughts. Above me the clouds like pearl shell began to glow with faint traces of crimson. Thickets of bamboo were growing near me and the green cane seemed darker but inside the thickets where the bamboo had broken the dead and yellow cane looked lighter than before.

I wanted to compose myself and yet I wanted to find answers to the questions by which I felt confronted. In my mind I believed in the Monster of Insanity that had hurled the flesh of men and the fire of the sun from a burning wound of stone and created the universe we knew thereafter. But deep in my emotions lay a refusal also as stubborn as stone to admit that nothing had meaning.

When I thought of Oola dying I also remembered what the Man of New Bodies had told me about her condition. Those words lay on my memory like the raised scars of initiation. Was death the initiation to life? I found myself standing. My thoughts were fathomless. They foundered in a bog. And all I had found by coming to this clearing was something I knew already. My emotions craved the meaning of a rocklike substance. They would have nothing to do with the slime of dissolution.

Breezes rose in the thicket and the slender tops of the bamboo waved in the wind and their narrow leaves of greenish gray stirred with the new motion. The wind seemed to be blowing from the Lake of the World and it reminded me that the air would blow into the long bamboo flute I had raised beside our house. I had thought that the sound of the wind playing music might soothe Oola and make her feel better.

I had waited too long and now I hurried to return to our house. No sooner had I entered the doorway than I found what I feared. Oola was surrounded by a crowd of relatives leaning over her or lounging by the doorway and blocking the air. Men sat against the walls smoking bamboo pipes and the whole house stunk of tobacco. They started to chant the moment I entered as though by doing so that I would feel embarrassed at throwing them out.

Between the words of the chant I heard the increasing hollowness

Davey

of Oola's deadened breathing. Oola's sister bent over her and tried to give her a drink but the water ran out of the side of her mouth. As she straightened up I saw the sadness on her face. She had not been recognized. "You will call me if you need me?" she asked. I nodded and watched her leave with the others. "Thank you," I called after her. Then she stopped and half turned around to make a sad, brief gesture.

I opened holes in the walls of the house to let the air in and I seized my bark cape and swung it back and forth to clear the smoke out. Then I raised Oola to a sitting position so that she could try to drink once more. "Can't you swallow?" She shook her head. I lowered her carefully and looked into her eyes. "Listen to me. You're going to get well. The Man of New Bodies is coming soon and he's bringing new magic. The new magic will make you well."

She nodded and put her hand on my arm, but the instant it lay there I told myself it weighed no more than a wren. We remained like that until the Man of New Bodies entered my house. He was preceded by a strange odor and he was carrying his string bag of mysterious leaves.

"I'm going to stay here," I said immediately.

"No! You're supposed to leave."

"I'm staying here."

"Then get me some fire and sit off to the side," he said grudgingly. His son began opening the bags. He spread banana leaves on the floor and on them he placed dried roots and fresh leaves and strange powders and plants. Some of the powders were so fine that he placed lighter leaves upon them so the air would not blow them away.

"I need two embers," he said to me in a surly tone.

"Then go get them."

His son went outside and returned with two glowing orange coals and placed them on a flat stone. The Man of New Bodies cut a root in two, laid it near an ember, and soon the odor of cinnamon spread through the growing darkness. Then he took another root and held it near Oola's nose and began talking as though in a dream.

"Breathe! Breathe! Breathe the smoke of the cinnamon! The smoke dislikes evil...the smoke dislikes children of evil..."

His voice seemed to come from far away. I did not like him but I knew he was my last hope. I tried to abandon doubt and as I stared at the embers glowing on the green stone I told myself that I must try to will this treatment into success. There would be nothing left if it failed and I found myself soundlessly repeating the words, 'Breathe! Breathe! Breathe the smoke of the cinnamon!'

Then I heard a hollow cough so dull and faint that it seemed not to come from a human.

"Get me some water," the Man of New Bodies demanded.

I passed him a small bamboo shoot and his son gave him the smoking end of a root which he placed in the water. For a moment we heard the water sizzle. Above the roof of palm fronds waves of heaviness seemed to be passing through the breezes and suddenly I realized it was the fleshy wings of fruit bats beating the evening air. Tonight there was something disgusting about it. I was sickened that above Oola flesh could fly away while lying here on the floor her own flesh prevented her from breathing.

The son looked at his father. "Do you want me to grind the mint leaves?"

"Yes. Since you're making the suggestions, go ahead. You have the grinding stones."

I leaned forward. This scent seemed to bring with it the promise of success. But again we heard a cough without air behind it.

"Father..."

"What?"

"We haven't tried the Relaxation of Dreams."

"Well, now that you're suggesting the magic, what do you have in mind, white dreams or black?"

"White ones, father."

"And how do you suggest to bring white dreams about in the dark?" A few minutes before he had placed something beside him and now he was sitting strangely upright. I moved quietly across the room and looked at him from the other side. Again I could see the tarry black saliva run from his mouth and down his chin. His son did not seem surprised by his father's selfishness and lack of control.

"Father, you're in the way," he said as he took over the treatment. He began crushing bark and leaves and I thought I was in a eucalyptus forest warmed by afternoon sunlight. I squeezed Oola's hand to reassure her.

But the Man of New Bodies sat more rigidly than ever and did not answer.

"I'll fix that!" I said.

I seized the old man by his bark belt and the hair of his head and dragged him across the floor and slammed him into a support post. Around us we felt the walls tremble. Then, as if nothing had happened, he began chanting with a voice like a ghost speaking through the mouth of a cavern.

"Flesh...flesh...you are evil. The evil of life is in you, Flesh." Despite myself the content of what he was saying compelled me to listen. His voice quavered and then became deep and his tones changed constantly like the light and the shadows flickering from torchlight.

"I lied," he chanted. "I lied to you, Manosoma." "All flesh is evil. Not only Child of the Lung. All lungs are evil. All flesh is evil. But dreams are not evil. Smoke is not evil. I lied to you, Manosoma," he repeated. "You know only war. What do you know of dreams? What do you know of smoke? Wood is the flesh of the tree and smoke is the soul of it."

I stood up and turned to his son. "Do you want me to kill him here? Or do you want to carry him back to your house?"

"I'll take him home," he said, shaking his head in embarrassment.

"Can I call you by your ghost name?" I asked him. "You have tried your best."

"Yes," he said quickly. "It's Youot."

"Good. I will give you the black pig with the smallest black stripe that I had promised your father." He began to make objections to this as we gathered his secret belongings and carried The Man of New Bodies outside. But in parting I told his son, "If my wife dies from his lack of care, I will kill your father immediately. A warrior can show him some things flesh can do! I will open his belly and strangle him with his own intestines."

I walked back slowly because I was haunted now by the thought that Oola had died. Through empty spaces between loosely woven walls of palm fronds I could see the orange lights of hearth fires burning. They were pleasant lights and they were warming people who were not dying.

Tentatively I knelt beside Oola and looked to see if her chest was moving and finally I heard the flatness of her breathing. She was alive! Gently I stroked her warm forehead. I told her the treatment had been a success and that she would have another one tomorrow. She had not said a word since the magic started but suddenly she surprised me by talking.

"…promise…" she seemed to be saying. I leaned down to listen. "…promise me…" she continued.

"I'll never say goodbye," I told her.

We exchanged love in our eyes. The effort seemed to have exhausted her and then silence followed and later, as much as I willed her to stay with me, she passed into the Next World.

17

Exhausted, I went back to sleep and this time I dreamed not of my wounds but of Oranooa's and I thought I had seen pass over his face a secret look of savage delight that had awakened a shadow of recollection fading now into sadness. Then I sensed he had roused himself from it but I imagined at the same time with his fingertips he touched those scars with a tenderness I had never seen exhibited toward the wounds of battle. It was not until later that the sound of chanting awoke me.

It was the Younger Man of New Bodies and with him he had two helpers.

"Magic roots in the earth," they sang. "Green leaves in the trees. White clouds in the sky. Blue water in the rivers, heal this man who called us. Then they blew into the dried stems of orchids and strange whistles came forth. "Birds on the branches," they sang. "Heal this man for he will owe us a tree kangaroo. Not a large tough one but a small tender one. Make his eyes white again like boars' tusks which have never seen smoke. Heal him! Heal him!" And then from a dry gourd they sprinkled over me the dust of mushrooms and suddenly my feet stung like fire and they were beating my soles with green nettles.

"Let the bad out of the bottom of this man's feet," they sang, but suddenly one helper jumped up because some tribesmen were about to enter the long house and he shouted, "Stay outside or this man will die. Do not dare to interrupt magic!"

They rolled me over and saw the camellia leaves that had been replaced on my wounds when I had first returned from The Sky of Stone. The Younger Man of New Bodies chanted, "Fruits of wild strawberries bleed on his wounds. Winds, blow away leaves from those with no knowledge," and again they turned me over. "Open your eyes," they commanded, and when I did I saw the six feet belonging to three monsters looking down on me, one with no mouth, one with no eyes, and the other with a face of a giant rat. Their voices sounded hollow behind their masks. "May he eat like a rat!" they shouted. "And then someone said, "Close your eyes," but no sooner had I done so than they poured a liquid on me and the liquid stung and made my flesh pucker and suddenly I had the taste of wild onions in my mouth. I squinted my eyes open without being told to do so and I saw them remove their masks and from net bags filled with many things they selected three tiny seashells and into my ears they blew three tiny blasts that I could barely hear.

The Younger Man of New Bodies shrieked, "Eat this! Eat this!" Then he stuck something between my teeth and more softly he called to me, "Chew! Chew!" And I gnawed on a root with a moldy taste and the three men waited while I went on chewing.

Then I couldn't stop talking.

"..." I said.

And three voices began singing and their sound was more beautiful than the song of a bird. "Hear him!" they sang. "Hear his words of white magic. The rivers will listen. The surf will stand still. Tell the world of this magic."

"..." I said again.

"Show us the leaves on your branches," they sang, and then I felt hands colder than stones and they wrenched my trunk from the earth. I lifted my arms and they turned into branches and leaves grew along them and the leaves glittered with light that was darkened but sparkling. Two twigs fell down and hung by my chest but around me green leaves moved in mixtures of starlight and sunlight.

Suddenly a drum beat and the orchid stems whistled once more.

"Drink this," they told me. "Trees can drink rain. No! Don't spill it! Where is your mouth?"

I tried to tell them. A tree does not need a mouth.

Davey

"Rustle your leaves again," they commanded.
I felt a small breeze move the boughs of my arms.
"More! Drink more!"
I was a tree with a mouth. Maybe I was a plant who eats flies.
"Now eat this," three winds from the forest told me. I heard them sighing in my branches. "Eat! Don't drink this one."
Then I knew if a tree has a mouth it must have a nose. For the air was filled with the raw smell from the underside of mushrooms. And I knew another thing also. A tree can hear its own shadow.
"Eat!" The winds chanted, and they turned into fingers and they held part of me open and their singing was more beautiful than before. Then they closed something and I heard voices throbbing with starlight in which no blood was beating and their song told me once more, "Eat it! Eat the flesh of the lotus. Eat the mushrooms of dreams."
"Now hold this under his nose," a voice commanded.
"Breathe!" the voice told me sternly.
Suddenly I had a stabbing sensation. Something had penetrated the bark I used for a nose. I felt the tree oozing and I managed to lift a branch upward and its leaves became wet. In the forest somewhere rain must be falling but the tree could no longer see and now I felt nothing. Was I growing in night or day? With the touches of feathers stone axes were chopping my trunk. I fell in the forest and was wrapped in wet bark. I lay near an orchid and the wind blew whistles out of the stem. Then the wind sang words and told something inside the forest, "Hold his head up. Open his mouth again."
And no sooner had the wind spoken than I became part of time and I turned from a tree into a stone and since blackness is the fate of stone inside me everything was black. But a mushroom grew from the stone and the mushroom glowed in the dark and the dark lightened and the stone turned into a man and the man opened his eyes.
No one was there. Legs that seemed like mine and arms that seemed like mine were trying to move. They were wrapped in the bark of the ti tree and I seemed to be lying on a soft layer of moss.

Brother of Cloud in the Water

Shadows surrounded me as though cast by a cavern but outside its entrance I saw light the color of amber.

Someone entered the cavern and squatted beside me.

"Brother of Cloud in the Water..."

I had heard that name before. My ears had escaped from the silence of stone. Another man came in and squatted also. I could hear them talking. I was glad my ears had returned from the land of silence, the second land that had followed the first. But I told myself it was my friendship with the ghosts that had prevented me from entering the first land where stones spoke and everything could talk. I sensed the sound would have killed me.

"You've begun to save him," someone said.

"Magic is saving him. Green dust living in dead mosses. White dust living under dead bark. Magic is working on him. Smelling the smoked venom of snakes and eating everything red. Like strawberries mixed into blood. He has been drinking blood, you know. The blood of bats."

"Yes. Through bamboo tubes. I see them."

"And bamboo makes arrows and bows to kill enemies. Let me look at him closer. Ah! Some skin is no good. See that? That needs more magic. Feel it. The fire is still in his flesh."

"I feel it. I can feel it now."

"Listen to me, Oranooa. You know what I need? I need the skin of a pig."

"If it's for him I have a pig you can use. He can owe me one. This man saved our tribe. He is a very great warrior."

"How can he pay me with a tree kangaroo and you with a pig?"

"He can pay you first. I can wait."

"You can? That will make magic easier."

"It is black inside a stone," I told them.

They ignored me. "This pig must be killed tonight. Skin it in the moonlight and bring it to me immediately. There must be no fire. This man is already on fire."

"I will do as you say."

"One more thing. Leave the fat on the skin. Then fold the fat inward."

"All right. Do you think you can save him?"

"Only my magic can save him. First he thought he was a tree. Now he thinks he is inside a stone, so the magic is working. Hold his head up again. Give me that bamboo tube again. There! Did you see him swallow?"

I gagged. Peppery fluid trickled down my chin and it too tasted like the milk of nettles. I lay there waiting for a dream to rise in the sky. Then I looked straight through the stone that continued to surround me and through the doorway I watched the sun glittering on the stars and the moon coming down from the night and once more I saw a silver breast shining and shadowed by secrets. But many dreams afterwards the stone turned to water and then into waves and one wave tried to crest but fell back and I wondered if I were the wave.

"Help him sit up," someone said.

Other men lifted me and I placed the palms of my hands on the floor and they kept me from falling. I saw a brindle piglet in the arms of a man and the little pig was smiling.

"Brother of Cloud in the Water," the piglet said.

"Who?"

"Brother of Cloud in the Water," the piglet repeated.

"Who do you want?"

"You! Your name is Brother of Cloud in the Water."

"Are you sure?" I demanded.

"Yes. And speak to me, not my pig," Saseve said to me.

So that was my name, I decided. Everyone said so. I saw men smoking pipes and suddenly the smell of tobacco reminded me of something.

"Then this isn't a stone?"

"No. This is the long house."

His words crawled through forests of hallucination and then like a python swallowed forgetfulness. I felt my memory return.

"The long house!" I exclaimed. "Again!" Near me I saw an old man wearing a necklace of purple beetles and as he leaned forward the firelight turned the violet into bands like rainbows gleaming suddenly upon the beetles' backs.

"Where is your green necklace?" I asked.
"Good! You remember my necklace. But do you know my name?"
"Oranooa," I replied.
"Do you know what just happened?"
I shook my head.
"Your life was fleeing like a wallaby before a fire of grass. Then your skin caught fire. Your flesh began burning. Your spirit made ready to leave your body like smoke. But magic is saving you. Magic put the fire out."

I remembered everything now. I knew who I was and who this old warrior was. On his other necklace each bright green beetle stood for a battle he had won and I told myself that I too had won many battles and maybe I had won even more. And despite my weakness I wondered whether I wished to end as he had with my battles turned into a necklace of beetles and my muscles turned into slackness and my strength wasted away.

"Oranooa?"
He inclined his head.
"Why did you not awaken me?"
"Awaken you! You were a visitor in the land of death. No one wanted to wake you. We wanted to give you time for your soul to reenter your body."

I looked across the room and I saw the husband of my wife's sister staring at me. In his hair he still wore one white cockatoo feather.

"Have the cockatoos screamed since my return?"
"No. And for good reason. The storm swept them away."

My memory had not totally come back, I decided. I had forgotten the storm and then I began to think that it might not be too soon to think that our situation could be dangerous. When the enemy tribe became brave enough they would want to avenge their leader. We had always encircled our village with tame cockatoos trained to sit in the trees and scream warnings. The birds knew our whistles and they were silent when we approached. They were tethered in the trees with one foot through a coconut shell to keep them from chewing the rattan cords that secured them. Now we would have to do something else. It takes a long time to train birds.

I leaned on one elbow. "Have the men make watch towers outside the village. Use the tops in broken trees and make platforms the older men can stand on during the day, not the warriors."

"All right. I will tell them." He gave me a shrewd and penetrating look. "You have almost come back from the fire of flesh and already you're worried."

I felt something inside me reflecting and I tried to put the reflections into words that would not distort the shape in which they had come to me.

"My worries are shadows. They are cast by the truth."

"I think you can see through the cloud of the future. You have the gift of doing that."

"Maybe."

I don't know how any days there were like that but there must have been many. At last I was able to walk and early one morning I went to see the Younger Man of New Bodies. He lived alone now in a house as round as the sun with a high roof that had extra rafters all across the top and from these rafters more plants were tied than ten men have toes and fingers. It did not smell like other houses that had odors of smoke and pigs and babies. Instead this house smelled as I remembered it when it was owned by his father and it was still permeated with eucalyptus and mint and mushrooms drying.

"You saved my life," I said.

He held his finger to his lips. Then he pointed to a wide smooth stone sprinkled with water. On the stones two snails were mating.

"We must whisper, Brother of Cloud in the Water."

"All right," I told him.

"Otherwise, we will disturb them."

"No doubt," I replied.

He glanced at me to see if I were being ironic.

"This may take a while. It's not what you may think."

"I never thought about it. Is it worth thinking about?"

"Yes. It is more interesting than men with women. Snails take half a day."

"That is not always true."
"About the men or the snails?"
I could tell from his question that he had no knowledge of love-making such as I had had so I shook my head. "It doesn't matter," I said.
Then he gave me a strange look and added, "But when they get through I will kill them."
"You always know what you are doing."
"Of course. But you must do something for me. I want you to take the ooze from the mating of the snails to your friend with no face. The man who is nearly an ancestor. Your friend who suffers from the Twilight of the Flesh. It is not good for a Healer of the Flesh to get near a body on which flesh dies while the body itself goes on living."
"I will be glad to do it."
"I knew you would. But try to whisper. Your voice is too loud. And there's one more thing. You owe me a tree kangaroo."
"Oh! All right. But that's all. Nothing more."
He stood up and walked outside. I followed him into the sunlight. He turned and I saw he was looking at my arms and my thighs.
"Your skin has healed well. That's good. My magic has won. My tree tea oil has driven away the sickness. My magic brought you back from the Forest of Bones."
"Yes. You magic is powerful."
He gave me a calculating look. "I have talked to Oranooa. If you can kill a tree kangaroo for me and a wild boar for him, you are strong enough to lead men in battle. But the magic makes me say one more thing."
"What does the magic say this time?"
"It says you must hunt by yourself."
"All right. But now something tells me you should know this. Your men must carry the animals back. I won't."
"Oh! I'll arrange that. Now listen to me carefully. Come back here when the sun is halfway into afternoon. I will have the snails ready."
On my way back to the long house I met twenty warriors leaving

on a raid and one warrior was armed only with a knife. But I saw it was a long sharp knife made from a human thigh bone and it could kill at close quarters. The other men were armed with thrusting spears and bows and arrows and they had sparrow down mixed with blood smeared on their forearms and shoulders. They knew it was bad to start a raid by stopping but they came over and clustered around me.

"We wish you were coming with us, Brother of Cloud in the Water."

"I will be with you soon," I replied.

Out of my waistband I withdrew the claw of the warrior animal and showed it to them. "It is a secret of magic," I told them. "It carries powerful magic."

Then I drew the man with the knife aside. "Do you know what to do?" I asked. He nodded firmly. But I made him tell me his plan in detail and then I let each man come close to me and touch the claw of the warrior animal. I could see it gave them confidence. At last I watched them walking in single file through a field of ferns and finally the wings of owls they wore in their hair seemed to give them the stealth and silence they wanted to absorb from the wings themselves and when the last wing disappeared down a hill all that could be seen were grasses and tall ferns.

I followed the directions of the Younger Man of New Bodies and waited till the sun was halfway to where it sank in the Lake of the World and as I entered his house I looked for the large flat stone and saw it was still damp but the snails had disappeared.

He handed me a small banana leaf wrapped with vines. "The snails are inside it without their shells. Now they are turned to magical slime. Tell your friend to rub them on his wounds." He put his hand on my forearm. "Tell him to let you know how it works and then you can tell me. Snails are creatures of magic. Some live in water. These lived on land."

I put the green package in a small net bag I had brought with me for just that purpose and I set out for the house of Anoogaro and his wife. He lived far away from the main village but he was in no danger. All he had to do was show his face to the enemy and they fled in fright. I had not seen him since I had brought the Woman With Hair the Color of Blood to meet him. Unlike some of our own people who had seen him and thought he was ghost which had had its face eaten off by a hideous beast in a dream, I remembered her kindness to both him and his wife.

It was a beautiful walk through the dry savanna and then up a high hill with a wide view of the Lake of the World lying below and flashing with sunlight in the late afternoon light. Above me the sky was as blue as the leaves of a tree that legends told us had a trunk as red as the blood of human beings. It has been seen by the dead and in dreams they have told us that the tree shed its bark not its leaves. Along its trunk lightning had thrown spears that left scars in the bark and if magic opened a man's ears then sometimes the scars would sing with voices that sounded like thunder.

18

"I have not yet seen such a tree, Forest Spring, but I have seen many magic things. I have seen my only brother disappear in The Pool that Forgets and reappear as a cloud. I have seen a huge warrior animal with a great golden eye. I have seen a Bird of Ghosts with hard silver feathers descend from the sky and bring special gifts for my tribe. I have seen a typhoon begin over The Lake of the World that has risen like a river python out of the water and then in a storm of bleeding bats and stinging snakes gently leave a soft beach of sand inside the stomach of the magic bird. I have slept in that sand beside a sand adder also sleeping and I have dreamt enchanted dreams of a woman who showed me her breast in the sky as she talked with the sound of flowers. I have even been one with A Woman With Hair the Color of Blood that I have seen drop from the sky and whose skin was white like that of our mourners. I have seen ..." But I stopped. I realized suddenly that seeds of remembered moments are always within reach and that such seeds can produce flowers of wisdom for the future.

In the days after my visit to Anoogaro I made it my purpose to climb the sides of mountains to recover my health and I made myself new spears and arrows. I spent many hours carefully drilling a hole through the claw of the warrior animal so that it would not split and when I had done so I strung it on the strongest fibers I could make into string. When I was ready I walked toward my favorite mountain, stopping only briefly to pull the creepers off the Bird of Ghosts. No matter how many times I removed them the vines left little circular sucker marks all over his silver skin. Then I continued upward and went straight to the rock where I had killed the warrior animal and I raised the necklace to the sky in the direction toward which he had vanished. He told me I could put the necklace over my head to wear around my neck and from that time on I have worn it constantly and have told myself that as long as I am alive I will never take it off.

Today, while I sit here on the moss I can see the sun and the moon are together in the sky above me. But mystery is everywhere and I know such sights must have a meaning for me. Both the sun and I have issued from a wound of stone but he has been hurled into the sky and I have remained on earth. He has died and been born every day while I have gone on living. But I have told myself that if I died his kind of death I might not rise from the darkness as he does each following morning so I have always kept my council when the old men among us discussed it. The young assume the old know about such things and the old do not betray that they are grateful for the assumption.

As a child I had felt it a duty to listen to forbidden talk and never admit I had done it. I knew long ago that some men thought they would turn into crocodiles whose eyes reflected our torches in the darkness and when the moon was full they would crawl onto the banks of the rivers and be nourished by moonlight. Now as I looked at this sleepy moon in the daytime sky I remembered when I was a boy the warriors had kept a sacred crocodile in a pen near the river and they had blinded him with spears and when his eyes no longer ran red with tears they tried to replace them with moonstones.

I had crawled through the grass that grew on one side of the long house and I lay without moving while I listened close to the wall. It could have meant death for me because boys are not supposed to know what goes on inside with the elders. But I have always been daring and I had grown up with death and I refused to be afraid.

I heard them talking about the crocodile. I recognized my father's voice as the first to speak.

"How long can this go on?" he asked. "Our enemies outnumber us. Yet four warriors and three men were killed capturing this crocodile. Today you can see seven skulls on the posts of the crocodile pen.

They are looking at their death inside it."

"It killed one man with a swish of its tail!" an astonished voice answered.

"I am not discussing what part of the crocodile killed anybody. I am discussing whether such magic is worth it."

Then I heard a rising murmur of disagreement as though some group were banding together against the speaker.

"It is our custom," a quavering voice declared.

"It may be our custom, but it is a custom which is killing us. For when we prepare the last two heads, there will be nine skulls on the crocodile pen, not seven. Two warriors were killed blinding it."

"Then today men lack the ability of yesterday," another old man proclaimed.

"Maybe so. But we are not through yet. We still must force moonstones into its eyes."

"That too is our custom! If the youth lack the daring and skill, let the older men do it."

Suddenly I heard angry voices and the young men shouted the old men down. Then the elders took refuge in offended silence but both sides waited for the first man to speak. I heard decisive steps creak on the floor and they sounded as though my father had withdrawn in disgust. Now the distance muffled some of his words.

" ..even if we do that..."

" 'If!'" an indignant voice shouted.

"All right. When! When we do that, what do we feed him? We can't use our own people."

"Do what our ancestors did. Feed him our enemies."

"So you want me to be your War Chief and yet you want to tell me when to make war."

"Who said that? Nobody told you when to make war."

"You just did! So make some other man Chief. Somebody who'll make war when your crocodile is hungry." A violent argument developed and I had crawled away with the sound of shouts still in my ears.

But today with the sunlight streaming from the blue sky and penetrating the rain forest, this memory faded with the others and I

Brother of Cloud in the Water

became conscious that I was staring at the moss around me. Near my feet a worm as flat as a leaf was noiselessly making his way toward spots of blue slime and white oozes of mildew that had formed on a wet piece of bark. His motion slower than a raindrop seeping through fibers of tree ferns seemed dreamlike and unaccustomed to daylight. Between outer edges of orange his body was marked by a broad streak of brilliant black that glistened in shade but when revealed in sunshine seemed almost to glitter with dark light. New thoughts began to enter my mind and this time they had nothing to do with war.

Yesterday I had had the warriors dress me for an important occasion, for no man can do that himself. When they were finished I went to my section of the long house and picked up my strongest bow and ten arrows tipped by splinters of cassowary bone notched forward so they could not be pulled back from whatever flesh they entered and a thrusting spear in case I had to fight at close quarters. None were bound by twine as a sign of peace. I wrapped some dried tree kangaroo meat in banana leaves and my friends came down the central aisle of the long house and watched me place the food in my string bag. They could no longer refrain from asking questions.

"Are you going hunting, Brother of Cloud in the Water? Why not take a bird arrow with three points? Why not take more?"

Then Saveve asked me, "If you are going hunting, why did you dress like the day of your marriage?"

I remained silent. I put my stone adz in my belt and I strode outside and they followed me. Women stopped and turned around as I went by and I saw the wide astonishment in their eyes. Nbugo came out of his house and my wife's sister followed him. He too plied me with questions me but she said nothing and instead she looked at me with eyes in which for the first time I saw a trace of sadness.

Everyone was staring at me. I had a long feather from the blue Bird of Paradise through the septum of my nose and the red tail feathers of palm parrots forming a crown on my head. They were tied tightly with wet fibers of rattan which would shrink and harden when dried. Above the tops of my biceps I wore bands of woven grass into which I intended to put flowers and under my knees the same bands of grass were woven also. But as a mark of something somber I wore between the red parrot feathers the dark wing of a charcoal owl. My friends had anointed my body with the red oils from pandanus seeds and in the strong sunlight I looked down at my thighs and my forearms and I saw flashes of crimson light.

Earlier I had sent the men to the Maker of Masks. I knew he would be in the shade, crouched over the wood as he carved lines in a new mask and from a distance I had seen him look up as they approached. From him the men had obtained three palm frond paint brushes and ochre from the earth and red stain from the special tree and the black charcoal from fires. Upon my forehead my friends had painted the green trunk of a sago palm with two fronds on both sides.

I wore a loincloth of golden cuscus skin and over it a tan bark belt stamped by blocks of wood which had been carved to leave the impress of skulls. I myself had rubbed charcoal dust into the indentations and now the belt was marked by a circle of black skulls. But I had wished to maintain the feeling of modesty and before me and behind me golden strands of short but thick netting covered my loincloth of cuscus fur.

As I left the village a stray sow tried to follow me but I hit her on the snout with a stick and shouted at her to go home. Then, as if she understood, she grunted and turned around, stopping occasionally to root in the ground, and started back toward the cooking fires. From the rear I could see her heavy teats swinging as she waddled away.

There were few clouds in the sky and after I had climbed out of the forest and started up toward the foothills I at last allowed myself to remember that it was on a day like this that Oola had died. She always did everything perfectly and she had even died on a perfect day. A breeze from the Lake of the World had started blowing and several times I stopped behind broad trees or tall tussocks of grass to make sure I was not being followed by a tribesman. But when I knew I was alone then I let my memory of her come back which had returned in starlight the night before and now in daylight it was still with me.

I kept my eyes open for enemies but at the same time the world seemed to imprint itself on my senses. There was even a fine smell here, the healthy smell of warm grass and a hint someplace of fragrance coming from flowers still hidden from sight. Ahead of me the blue mountain ranges rose from the foothills and shimmered above the heat waves moving slightly over the ground. I saw two hawks sailing in slow circles widening and then coming together and widening again in a breeze no longer filled with smoke from the village. There were no people and nothing but the land and above it the sky. The wind died down but ahead of me the grass kept moving and I knew it must be a grass python crawling toward the shade. I followed his curving movements and then I saw him stop and he curled his head around and looked at me. He was very beautiful and the sunlight glistened on his body and formed the colors of a rainbow. He looked almost wet there in the dry grass and he had no scales over his eyes so I knew he had just shed his skin. Finally we parted. He disappeared in the undergrowth and I went on walking toward the distant summits.

I was approaching a high savanna and the dry plain inclined upward and led on toward the hills which themselves led toward the mountains. The first two mountain ranges in this direction still belonged to my tribe but I knew that we had not yet admitted even to ourselves that the third range was in dispute. I did not expect to meet enemies this far toward the mountains we still controlled but there was always a chance that enemy hunters might be trying to combine hunting with scouting in order to report to their war chief how strong we were in our own land. Perhaps I had delayed these ideas by leaving the smoked body of their last fight leader where he could not be missed. Suddenly I smiled to myself. Tall Grass and I had given him the deadly jade-colored blood from the green skink and before he knew it the end had come. So that is why I did not carry a bird arrow in my hand but only arrows intended for men.

New sights began to claim my attention. Around me the grass was growing only as high as my waist and as I walked along I saw more sudden movements in it and then wallabies leaped from cover and in great convulsive hops, jumped to the right or left trying to escape me. Even though I wasn't hunting them, they acted as

Davey

though I had them cornered. Their coats of soft brown fur appeared suddenly in the air above the grass and then disappeared beneath it. One leaped high enough that I could see a baby wallaby looking back at me out of the pouch of its mother who had gray hairs all over her face and streaks of gray on her hind legs. The old mother made another gigantic leap but it was less high than the first one and I could tell she was tiring. When I paused she instantly stopped leaping but continued taking little tired hops away from me into the separate tussocks of dried grass. I knew she wanted to return to the greener area with softer leaves and I waited while she hopped more and more slowly toward the protection of some shrubs. For a few minutes I stood still so that she could regain her breath.

When I began walking again I saw long broad lines dragged in the dust by her thick and worn tail. Immediately I knew that something was occurring in my mind that was different now than it had been in the past. When I had hunted long ago I would have wanted to kill such an old wallaby mother and her child. She would have been easy to shoot and then I could have killed her infant quickly with a stone club. I told myself that if I had been starving today, I would be preparing a meal of wallaby meat right now. But my wounds have healed and other hunting has prevented famine so even though I remembered a time or two when I had been reduced to eating the sour red berries from mangrove trees, today I was not hungry. That was just as well for the wallabies had disappeared and around me I saw twigs stripped of leaves and small mushrooms growing out wallaby droppings that were producing an unpleasant smell. It was not an enjoyable place so I started climbing again but I had to be careful where I walked for growing among the stones were small gray cactuses as round as pebbles.

Before me the purple mountains rose higher and after a while I stopped and slipped the net bag from my shoulder. I knew the place and I remembered that this was the point at which I had laid Oola's body down and I began to appreciate the passion I had experienced and the physical effort I had made to carry her all the way up here. This time I wanted to stop and think before I climbed the last little hill on which I had constructed her grave. So I looked back at the path I had taken this time and the path I had taken before and this pause afforded me a chance to remember personal times and so postpone the eventual encounter with her grave despite the fact that this was the sole reason I had made this journey.

Below me I saw the varying shades of green on the different tree tops forming the height of the rain forest and through it ran silver lines of rivers that fanned out into broad areas of tan silt and salt water. Past the widening deltas the darker blue waters of the Lake of the World stretched far away. Thin clouds as lacy as mimosa had appeared in the sky and they sailed with slow delicacy briefly across the sun. But soon it broke clear and then an invisible wave surged somewhere on the incoming tide and suddenly rays of light glittered from the moving surface of the water. And I was reminded now of our widows waving their hands at the setting sun which protects the souls of the dead living in the spirit world beyond. Fresh breezes swirled upward off the savanna and my headdress of parrot feathers waved in the wind and the motion brought me back to the present and reminded me why I had worn it. I had come to visit Oola.

"So our talk has been good for me, Forest Spring. I had planned to visit with my wife in our special way and then get in my canoe, smear myself with turtle blood to attract the sharks which control the lies around us and jump into the Lake of The World to combat such things, never to return to this island except in spirit. Now..."

I grew tired of lying on the moss and shifted my position so that I could sit down on a log. A sudden movement caught my eye and made me turn my head to find a black and white dog from the village approaching me with caution. He stood stiffly, staring at me, as though he could not decide whether to bark or lie down. Above us the clouds were so thin I could see straight up through them and once in a while the fronds of palm trees creaked and then grated in the sudden breezes.

From my hidden spot I could see the long house higher than the bodies of twenty men and could almost make out the designs painted in ochre and maroon mixed from red clay and outlined by edgings of soot. Men whose fathers had taught them these things devote their lives to the decorations of our shields and masks and also carve human bones in the sacred image of insanity, the creator of the contradictions of our universe. I sighed. These are my people. And just as with my father I am constantly being challenged by adult children who never doubt their current knowledge and resent the acquisition of it. Their spoken and unspoken criticisms for my not having the power to bring forth another Bird of Ghosts is ongoing and unavoidable but what am I to do? I have not told them that their disapproval directs my reflection which instigates my curiosity to understand what others have not yet grasped. The only things I cannot condone are lies about me spoken by small minds and jealous souls and these I must continue to combat.

"Besides, Forest Spring," I said on a lighter note, "these men belong to a very old group, in fact as old as myself. Their sole requirement for initiation is not to know what they are talking about. I've always thought it's a pleasure to know that a friend lost is an enemy gained."

In the searing heat my eyelids grew heavy since sleep has avoided me for days like the wings of a bat, and I wondered if nighttime were the only time that warriors were right to regard themselves as better than other men.

"I am a warrior, Forest Spring, and I do not regret that I could be nothing else."

The quiet of the moment lifted acceptances formed in other daylight hours from my spirit and it occurred to me that at night nothing is expected by sleepers from men who are awake. I realized that in the past years I have unconsciously grown to like that and it is the reason I have often found myself waiting to steal silently into the night and be alone with thoughts which in daylight I would not have allowed to remain.

I looked over at the dog lying near by. It began to seem odd to me that a warrior who cannot sleep and a dog which always sleeps have come together without wanting to do so. But at night such thoughts of mine seem neutral and my mind feels as free of blood obligations as the flight of moths in the forest. In fact, I told myself, my mind is as free as an owl because an owl hunts in the darkness and his hunting often ends in death whereas my thoughts do not always do so.

"I will disavow this next thought if you repeat it, Forest Spring, but these words hint at the sadness of our world being greatly involved with killing. It is unfortunate that in a world filled with the beauty of birds and butterflies and orchids that men feel they need to kill. I have wondered in my dreams what it would be like if instead of knives made from the thigh bones of enemies each warrior had the tooth of a possum and could carve something lasting and color it with ochre from the earth itself. But in daylight I know the truth remains that for my tribe to survive, our warfare between headhunters and cannibals needs to be ceaseless. So I have decided that I should not leave just yet. As you have been quietly listening it has given me a chance to reconsider my plans. I do not want my skull to end up on a dusty shelf in anyone's long house but the fact is we do live in a land of death and a soundless voice is implying that my life is a forest through which the trails have been blazed with only one reason. I am Chief of the People of the Only World. They are threatened with extinction and my purpose, as was my father's, is to keep them alive."

Flights of fruit doves were passing over the forest and faint traces of smoke drifted toward me from houses in the village. The dry season has come and the occasional silence of the forest is broken by the evening hooting of boobook owls. My fingers seemed to raise themselves to touch my headdress which I have yet to remove. Even the feathers of our Birds of Paradise impart a feeling of soft glory from which even death is not able to remove the beauty.

I finally stood up.

"I'll be back, Forest Spring. I'm going to fix the wind flute."

Both the dog and I walked back to my house and I stopped a moment beside the fire that Oola's sister had begun to start for me each evening. The embers had fallen into a hole where they would keep burning and I covered them with a rock, but I left one edge slightly open. Then I reached for the pole to which I had tied a long section of slender bamboo. If I raised my hands over my head I could twist the bamboo in the direction the wind was blowing and as it was no sound came from it so I knew it was facing in the wrong direction to play music. I had cut slits between the nodes of the bamboo and toward the bottom I had cut wider openings. Now I waited a moment so that I could feel the movement of the wind and at last I felt it blowing from where the sun sets in the Lake of the World.

The bamboo was bound tightly by the rattan on the pole and I had to rotate it hard to get it into the right position. Once more I found myself staring up at the stars and what looked like clouds of stars also. The smell of pigs and blossoms drifted to me but thankfully the odor from the animals faded first and I was left with the sweetness of night blooming flowers. Suddenly the sides of the bamboo slits caught a gust of wind and I heard music blowing from the flute. I stood still, charmed by the beauty around me. Despite its covering of stone, insects had been drawn to the fire and occasionally I heard the swoosh of nighthawks diving among them. Finally I moved toward my darkened doorway.

There will always be time to take my canoe out on the Lake of the World, I whispered almost to myself. I had just remembered something important. Something that I had almost told the Woman With Hair the Color of Blood. Many truths could be lies which have not been discovered.

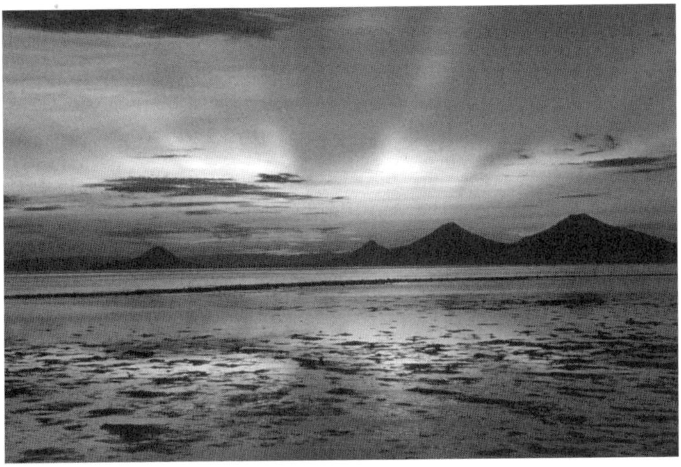